Dark Designs

STEFANIE SPANGLER

Unlocking New Worlds

Dark Designs
Copyright © 2017 by Stefanie Spangler All rights reserved.
First Print Edition: May 2017

Print ISBN-13: 978-1-940215-97-6
Print ISBN-10: 1-940215-97-8

Red Adept Publishing, LLC
104 Bugenfield Court
Garner, NC 27529
http://RedAdeptPublishing.com/

Cover and Formatting: Streetlight Graphics

This is a work of fiction. Names, characters, places, and incidents either are the product of the author's imagination or are used fictitiously, and any resemblance to locales, events, business establishments, or actual persons—living or dead—is entirely coincidental.

For my dad, who was always ready with a bedtime story, and my mom, who looks for the everyday kind of magic.

Chapter One

I F LIVESTOCK HAD EVER LIVED on the farm, the animals were gone
long before Ivy and Violet came to live there. Lately, the only critters
that occupied the stalls of the dusty barn were the cats and their tiny,
elusive prey. Jack Grant had always told his granddaughters that a farm
needed "good mousers," so eight-year-old Ivy thought they were practically
as useful as a cow or horse would have been. She didn't see any reason to
keep other animals on the small Midwestern farm.

Ivy's twin sister, Violet, raced into the barn. The dirt floor had long
since been ground to a soft powder, but she still made enough noise to
startle the kittens. Violet always ran, even when she had no reason to hurry.
Once, she'd told Ivy that she liked to imagine flying like a bird when she
ran. Ivy had no doubt that Violet had spent the entire morning outside,
taking advantage of warm weather that promised to turn to sweltering heat.

Violet's sneakers thumped across the floor of the barn to the stall where
Ivy had nestled. "Ivy, Gran said she's going to town in about an hour, and
do you wanna go?" Violet choked a little as she inhaled a mouthful of
dust that her footsteps had stirred up. Static electricity lifted layers of her
ponytail in the dry air.

"Shhhh…" Ivy hissed as if she were an adult addressing a child. "You're
bothering the kitties." She turned back to the kittens, intent on ignoring
Violet's intrusion.

Violet crouched beside her and delicately petted a kitten with gray
stripes. It mewled quietly then yawned before returning to its nap. "So you
wanna go? I'm gonna go." She bounced on her toes as she squatted, as if
deciding whether or not to stick around for Ivy's answer.

Ivy stared at the kittens. The warm spring breeze already threatened to melt away into sweltering summer heat. She couldn't stay in the barn all day. "Yeah, I'll go."

Violet sprang to her full height, making Ivy flinch and earning a whine from the kitten in her hand. "Okay! I'll go tell Gran. She said be inside in fifteen minutes to clean up, 'cause she's leaving at eleven with or without you." With their grandmother's instructions barely out of her mouth, Violet was off, running toward the house.

Ivy gave each of the kittens a last snuggle in hopes that they would remember her once they opened their eyes. Kittens that didn't enjoy being petted and carried around the yard were no fun.

Slowly, she became aware of another presence in the barn. Her eyes roamed away from the kitten cradled in her arms to the boots standing just beyond the stall door, next to her discarded sandals. Eyes wide, she sprang to her bare feet as fast as she could without trampling the kittens.

Charlie Logan was blocking the way out of the stall. The sunlight that slipped in through the gaps in the barn's wooden planks cast his face in mottled stripes. She knew him because Grandpa Jack had always let his granddaughters roam the farm freely, and Charlie had spoken to her many times. Never alone, though. She stood awkwardly, her eyes darting around the dimly lit solitude of the barn.

"Nice kittens you got there." He nodded cheerfully toward the kittens then smiled. His hand twitched as if he might reach out and touch her.

"Yeah," she said quietly, looking back and forth between Charlie and the kittens. "None of them are sick or anything. Sometimes there are sick ones..." Ivy rambled nervously until her eyes settled on Charlie's face, and then she stilled, wishing she could disappear.

Charlie moved in closer, trapping her in the corner of the stall. "They'll all be good mousers, I bet."

His tone was friendly, but Ivy's guts tensed. She desperately wanted to be away from the stall that had, without warning, become too dark and far too secluded. If she shouted, someone would likely hear her and come, but Charlie had always seemed nice enough. Maybe he did just want to talk about kittens, and she didn't want him to get in trouble for not being busy at work.

When she made a move toward the door, his tall frame shifted. She jerked back, away from his body, pushing herself tighter into the corner of the stall. He was close enough that his scent of stale cigarette smoke and sweat forced its way into her nostrils and stomach. When he exhaled, his breath smelled of strong coffee.

In slow motion, Charlie reached out and touched her hair just over her ear. Heart in her throat, she froze. Charlie Logan had not come to discuss anything good. He smiled at her affectionately as he stroked her hair.

"I need to go." She gushed the entire sentence as if it were a single word. "I'm supposed to go with Gran."

She willed herself to move, but at her smallest motion, he leaned forward, pressing himself against her. Wishing she could sink into the rough sycamore planks behind her to keep from coming in contact with his body, she squeezed her eyes shut, pinching droplets of tears from the edges of her eyelids. She opened her mouth and tried to call for help, but the blood rushed so loudly in her ears that she wasn't sure if any sound had escaped. He leered down at her wordlessly. His heat seeped into her everywhere that his body touched hers. The front of his T-shirt was damp with sweat, and her stomach clenched in revulsion. He started breathing heavily. His fingers tangled in her hair, and her heart threatened to jump out of her throat. His grin turned to a snarl. Then his eyes widened, and his back went rigid.

"You slide on out of there, Ivy," Grandpa Jack said from behind Charlie.

Relief mixed with confusion washed over her. She had been so absorbed in the closeness of Charlie's body that she hadn't noticed her grandfather's approach. Charlie apparently hadn't heard him, either. He was stock-still. She jerked her head, wincing as her hair caught in his grip. His fingers loosened. She scrambled away from him then clutched at her grandfather's arms, which were holding a pitchfork to Charlie's back.

Without looking at Ivy, Grandpa Jack shook her off gently. "You go on in the house."

Charlie's T-shirt dimpled under the pressure of the tines.

She backed out of the stall and toward the barn door. Hiding just inside the entrance to the final stall, Ivy breathed in the dust that sparkled in a shaft of sunlight. A gap in the boards offered a view of her grandfather's back and the motion of his pitchfork.

Charlie tried to twist to face Jack, but the older man increased the pressure of the tines, forcing him forward into the wall. "We were just talking about cats is all. It's hot outside, and I thought it'd be cooler in here. Just takin' my break."

"I *ever* lay eyes on you—on my farm or anywhere else—again, I will kill you." Grandpa Jack's dead-calm voice sent a shiver through Ivy. "I will kill you. I will put you in the ground." Jack released the fork just enough for Charlie to twist around and face him. "You get this one last chance to get gone."

"You can't run me out of town just for talking to a little girl." The bravado in Charlie's voice faltered at the end. "You don't get to treat people like that."

Jack didn't move. Ivy had never thought of her grandfather as mean, but she recognized his tone of voice. He was not making an idle threat. Grandpa Jack's jaw was tight. The tendons in his neck stretched his weathered skin.

Could Grandpa Jack really kill somebody? Ivy held her breath. The men were silent and still.

Finally, Charlie squeaked, trying to take a breath. He put his hand on the metal shaft to shove it away. But Jack forced the fork into Charlie's ribs.

"You get gone, or I'll kill you now." Jack's control over his obvious rage only made him more menacing.

Charlie paled and drooped over the pitchfork, but Jack jerked him upright. Ivy covered her mouth to stifle a gasp. After casting a sidelong glance at the kittens, she turned and ran. Ivy had never enjoyed running as much as she did at that moment.

Audrey Grant was putting clean dishes into the cabinets when Ivy burst into the room, gasping. The screen door banged shut, and the child stood bent over with her hands on her knees. The shimmering cloud of anxiety surrounding Ivy told Audrey that the girl was not simply in a hurry, excited about a trip into town.

Frowning, Violet jumped from her perch on the counter. She leaned down next to Ivy and gently patted her back. "Ivy…" she whispered, "are you okay?"

Ivy clutched Violet and started to sob in short, choked breaths. The two girls sank to their knees together in front of the door. Over Ivy's shoulder, Violet looked to Audrey for direction, her eyes wide with confusion.

Audrey knelt next to them and gently peeled Ivy's arms off Violet. She grasped Ivy's shoulders. "Sweetie, slow down. Breathe." Audrey took her own slow, deep breaths to demonstrate. "What happened?"

As Ivy gathered her composure, Audrey wiped the girl's eyes with the dishcloth she'd tossed over her shoulder.

"I was in the barn, and Charlie came to talk about kittens, and then he was really close to me and touching my hair." Her voice cracked as she gestured vaguely toward her hair. "He was really creepy, and I couldn't get away. But Grandpa's out there with him, and he has a pitchfork. I don't know what happened. He was there, and then Grandpa was there…" She shook her head, her lip quivering.

Audrey pulled Ivy against her chest and embraced her. "He only touched your hair?" Audrey hoped her voice didn't reveal that she was overwhelmed with fear and anger, thinking of what could have happened. "Nothing else, right? Just your hair?"

"Yeah. He was kind of smooshing me into the wall." Ivy put a hand on Audrey's hair to demonstrate what Charlie had done. "But if Grandpa hadn't come… he was really close. I don't know…" A small hiccup swallowed her words.

Audrey wasn't certain Ivy had fully understood the man's intent. Through the screen door, Audrey's eyes locked onto the barn a few yards from the house. She groped blindly for Violet with her free arm. When the girl grasped it, she pulled her in and hugged both of her granddaughters. Then she wrapped Ivy's arms around Violet's shoulders. Audrey jumped to her feet and ran out the door, careening between the sharp, ragged edges of relief and fury. She didn't hear the door bang closed behind her, so she knew the girls had followed her to the porch.

She whirled, pointing at the house. "You stay here."

They both froze in the doorway.

Audrey started across the yard. She wasn't sure if she was going to the barn to stop Jack from doing something he would regret or if she was going to do something regrettable herself. Her shaking hands felt hot. Her ears burned. The heat outside only fueled her internal flames. She imagined strangling Charlie Logan and hitting him so hard that he fell to the ground. The magic coursing through her hummed across her palms, so close to the surface.

Then Charlie emerged from the barn, freezing Audrey in her path. Sudden realization about his appearance curdled her blood. Young and handsome, he was tall, dark, and well muscled—a wolf in sheep's clothing. Maybe that was why she hadn't noticed he was capable of something so ugly—because he wasn't outwardly unattractive. Though tempted to use every ounce of power she had, Audrey tamped it down into the hollow of her stomach. *Too many eyes.*

In that moment of hesitation, her anger felt displaced. Audrey knew she was as much to blame. Charlie was only a wolf being a wolf. *But I should have seen it.* She cursed herself, remembering flashes and small actions that had given him away. Audrey had ignored her intuitions and made excuses for him. *My fault,* she thought, pushing away the image of her daughter's face, along with memories of the signs she'd ignored then, too. *I'm to blame—again.*

Her vision narrowed until she saw only Charlie Logan. She followed several paces behind him. She didn't know what had transpired in the barn between Jack and Charlie, but watching him walk awkwardly to his truck, she knew who had been wielding the pitchfork. When Charlie got inside the vehicle, Audrey stopped a few feet away from the bumper. He tried to light a cigarette with shaking hands before tossing it aside in frustration. Then he smashed the key into the ignition and started the truck. They made eye contact for an instant, and her stomach twisted with anger—at them both.

The gravel dust that stirred up along the long driveway partially concealed his retreat. Audrey stared after it, forcing her heart to beat a normal rhythm.

"No, it's all right, Sam," Jack called out.

She turned to see Jack leaning against the doorjamb of the entrance to the barn, his arms crossed over his chest. Their head farmhand jogged to a stop next to Jack, his eyes darting from the dust cloud to Audrey. She started over to them as Jack spoke to Sam, waving him back toward the orchard. With a nod, Sam walked slowly toward the trees before casting a glance back over his shoulder.

"Were you goin' to beat on him or something?" Jack asked her with wry smile.

"I thought about it." Her anger was swiftly deflating into relief, and the thrum of energy in her hands dissipated. "What did you say to him?"

"Told him I'll kill him if I see him again." The simple, concise statement hung heavy in the air as Audrey's eyes met his. "I poked him a little." He nodded toward the pitchfork resting in its place near the door.

Audrey surveyed the pitchfork for a second before her gaze returned to her husband. "Would you really?" She looked at him hard. "Kill him, I mean."

His forehead wrinkled with contemplation. Then he looked away, swallowing hard, a grimace flashing across his face. "He'd already be dead if I'd turned up a few minutes later." Eyes shining with unacknowledged tears, he pushed himself away from the barn and straightened. He glanced at the house and at the girls watching from the porch, then he turned to walk back to his work. Over his shoulder, he said, "And a man who's done that doesn't come back with nothing good in mind."

Audrey returned to the house with deep resolve. She had failed to trust her instincts for the last time. The girls needed to know they were special, that they could protect themselves and each other.

Chapter Two

CHARLIE'S HEART POUNDED TO THE beat of a fierce excitement. Some things he did because he was driven by an unnamed, persistent force from within. Other things he did because he enjoyed them. He craved the rush of adrenaline that came with raw defiance of the rules. Years had passed since he'd felt such a rush… nearly a decade. Jack Grant wasn't around to steal his prize this time.

He looked around the darkened room. The owner of the grand house was away—on a trip that Charlie knew he himself would never take and probably driving a car that Charlie would never be able to afford. The paintings on the wall meant little to Charlie Logan, except that he understood other people would pay to own them. Breathing in the heavy scent of the owner's cologne, he imagined the amount of time a man would have to spend in a room for it to take on his scent. This other man would surely place his valuables there, where he could keep them close to him.

The house had an alarm system, as most expensive homes in the area did. However, the house hadn't always been so elaborate. The neighborhood was a cluster of historical homes that had been remodeled, reshaped, and resized. But the window to the storage room in the garage had been long forgotten by the homeowners and security company alike.

Instead of blindly breaking in, Charlie had taken the time to educate himself about the home, even going so far as to pose as an electrical company employee just to get an up-close view. He had failed to plan plenty of times before and had resolved not to make that mistake again. Savoring his victory over the alarm system, he'd taken his time exploring the house. His friend Artie waited outside in a car parked on the street, where the ornate lampposts were more decorative than luminous.

This house has got to have a safe. Even though the paintings were too large to be his first haul away from the house, he gingerly pulled one away from the wall to check behind it. Nothing. He turned to survey the entire room.

Suddenly, headlights flashed through the window. He froze for a brief second as the lights passed over him, then he hustled in a crouch to the window ledge. From there, he saw the garage door open. *Oh, shit!*

His eyes darted around the room, looking for something he could take with him on a mad dash from the building. He refused to leave empty-handed. Squatting behind the desk, he spotted a key stuck to the bottom of the desk chair. He peeled it off and jammed it into the nearest keyhole—in the bottom drawer of the desk. The key fit but didn't turn in the lock.

The sound of the garage door sliding closed filled him with another thrill of panic as he shifted his gaze around the room, searching. He scrambled away from the chair, tripping over the edge of the mat, which sent him sprawling across the floor. He jerked the mat in anger, inadvertently revealing another keyhole. *It* has *to be that one.*

Relief and self-satisfaction poured over him as the key clicked into the lock of what turned out to be a safe hidden in the floor beneath the desk. Hoping for jewelry or cash, he pulled back the safe's hatch. He found nothing but a wooden box about the size of a large textbook.

"Dammit," he muttered. His head snapped up as he heard cheerful voices from a few rooms away. Laughter floated toward him, along with the glow of lights from the other room. *Gotta get gone.* The box had to hold valuables of some kind to warrant storage in a hidden safe, so he snatched it up and clutched it to his chest. Its weight reassured him that it held *something* at least.

He opened the window and leaned heavily into the screen. It gave way with no more sound than a metallic snick, but the peal of an alarm told him his exit hadn't gone unnoticed. He tumbled into a hedge but immediately righted himself. After a sprint across the yard, he threw himself into the car with Artie.

"Go!" he shouted.

Artie turned the ignition and jammed the car into gear. As the vehicle crept away, Charlie looked back at the house. Every light was on. He and Artie grinned at each other.

While Artie drove, Charlie rode in silence. Still giddy, he couldn't think of anything but getting the box open. Artie might have tried to start a conversation, but Charlie ignored him. The half-hour ride seemed to take an eternity. As soon as the car stopped at Artie's one-bedroom house crammed between a couple of dumpy sheds at the edge of the woods, Charlie was out, stalking across the weedy lot, Artie on his heels like an eager puppy.

Artie jogged ahead to open the ramshackle door to his house then ushered Charlie inside. Charlie set the plain wooden box on the table, and they stared at their odd prize for a moment.

Pulling at the small padlock on the delicate clasp, Artie said, "No problem to cut this off, Charlie." His eyes glimmered with his need to please Charlie.

But Charlie waved him off. With a sharp yank, he snapped the entire clasp off the box. "Not exactly Fort Knox there, Art." He sniggered as Artie's mouth sagged into a frown.

"Not hardly worth the padlock, man."

Charlie hesitated to open the box, feeling suddenly that revealing the contents should be a momentous occasion. After casting a sidelong glance at Artie, he lifted the lid.

Right away, Charlie could tell the book was important—it vibrated with power. After releasing the book from its prison, he gingerly pressed his finger to the brass buckle that held it tightly closed. Some of the pages had long since come free of the binding and were in place only because of the strap.

"Wow," Artie whispered.

With a sneer, Charlie cast a sidelong glance at him. Charlie wasn't exactly smart, but he was just smart enough to talk other people into thinking he was. Arthur Bavery was no exception. Charlie had ideas, and Artie always thought the newest idea was going to be the one that made them both rich. So he'd hitched his cart to Charlie's horse a few years earlier.

Since giving up on any kind of honest work, Charlie had tried his hand at several occupations from conman to drug dealer. Conning had gone all right—not great but simply all right. When it had come to drugs, he didn't have the guts to sell the hard stuff, and he'd had too much competition selling weed. After Jack Grant had run him out of Oak Hill, Charlie returned home to Ohio, where he wasn't welcome but was at least tolerated.

Even after Charlie's own mother sent him packing, Artie had stuck with him. *Maybe that loyalty is about to pay off for ol' Art…*

In a huff, Charlie shoved beer cans and unopened mail off Artie's kitchen table.

Artie stooped in a halfhearted attempt to catch a can. "C'mon, man," he whined as the cans clattered to the floor, spilling their dregs on the envelopes.

"Oh, shut up." Charlie lifted the leather book out of the box and laid it in the place he'd cleared. He undid the buckle, his fingers threatening to turn shaky. The pages were yellowed, and several were scorched as if burnt by sparks strayed from a flame. He flipped past drawings of plants, rocks, and phases of the moon done in smeared ink. Scribbled handwritten notes filled any would-be blank spaces. He could practically feel the many hands that had held the book.

When Artie reached out to touch a page, Charlie shoved his hand away. "Hey, this is delicate stuff here, Art. Quit getting all grabby with it."

"It seems like something good, right, man?" Artie's voice reminded Charlie of a child waiting for approval from a teacher.

The book's power seeped into Charlie's fingertips as he nodded. "Definitely, Art." A smile spread across his face. "Our luck's about to change."

Chapter Three

IVY TURNED OFF THE PAVED road and onto the gravel drive that led up to the house where she had lived most of her life. The backseat and trunk of her car were filled with all the belongings that she could call her own. Only the roof of the house was visible as she drove along the line of apple trees that flanked the road. The gleaming white farmhouse with its wraparound porch and dark-blue trim stood guard over the orchard. Rounding the curve of the drive, she expected to see Bev or Sam in the yard of the smaller house, which Grandpa Jack had always called "the farmhand's house." But the yard was empty.

Forcing herself to look away from the barn, she studied the house, where sunlight sparkled on framed mirrors hung over the doors. Mixed emotions swirled through her.

School was finished. After four years, her official homecoming had arrived, and she was the proud holder of a bachelor's degree in business management, class of 2005.

Whatever that even means. There wasn't exactly much business to manage in Oak Hill. Violet, with her associate in agricultural business management, was already handling the farm. *What does that leave for me?* Ivy wondered, but she knew that her decision to return had more to do with the specter of her mother than it did with career opportunities.

She sometimes felt that she and Violet lived in a vacuum of information about their mother. Her grandmother rarely spoke of Rachel, and Ivy assumed Gran simply never thought about her. Jack had often talked about her, recalling his memories of her childhood, but he'd never spoken of her in the present tense. He seemed settled in the idea that she had died. Maybe the feeling of closure had given him peace. Ivy couldn't share that peace.

The tires of her blue Cavalier crunched over gravel as she rolled to a stop. The car was surely coated in dust from its trip down the driveway, something that rarely happened while it was parked on campus. The dust reminded her of her grandfather. *Grandpa Jack never would have stood for me showing up in a dirty car.* She smiled at the thought, which tugged at her heartstrings. She wished Jack were waiting for her at the house, too, instead of just her grandmother and sister. Knowing he wouldn't be at her college graduation had cemented her choice not to attend the ceremony.

Violet came out of the barn and crossed the yard, headed for the house. Her white T-shirt and denim shorts with work boots made her look every bit the quintessential farm woman. Her long dark hair was pulled up into a knot at the back of her head. As she waited for Ivy to exit the car, Violet held up an arm to shield her eyes from the afternoon sun that drenched the countryside.

"So you're back, then." Violet smiled slyly. "Gran was planning a trip up to get you on Saturday."

Ivy pushed her sunglasses to the top of her head as she stepped out of the car. "My friends were pretty much gone already, and it was boring." She waved an arm at the car. "Plus, all of my stuff fit in my car. I didn't need you guys to bring the truck. So I decided to just come home." Really, she'd been so anxious about moving home that she'd been desperate to get it over with. *I'll miss Rhiannon, though. I should call her...*

"Yeah, I knew you would, especially since you're skipping graduation. Gran didn't believe me." Violet rolled her eyes. "Let's go see Gran, and we'll get your stuff later." She waved Ivy up the brick path toward the house.

With a sigh, Ivy grabbed her purse from the car and followed her sister. Bluegrass music and the smell of baking bread met them at the door.

Their grandmother was at the sink, singing loudly. She turned to dry her hands on the towel that hung from the oven-door handle. "Oh, good grief!" She covered her heart with her hands. "You scared me to death, sneaking up on an old woman like that." She gathered Ivy into her arms, hugging her tightly.

"Hey, Gran." Ivy returned her grandmother's squeeze. "I was afraid you would be mad I was home early."

Audrey held her at arm's length by the shoulders and looked into her eyes intently. "No! I'm not mad. It's wonderful! You're here, and I don't mind how that happens, just as long as you're here." She smiled and squeezed Ivy again.

Violet wandered over to the oven. She inspected the contents of the hot cookie sheet on the countertop. "Oh, it's pretzels. Not bread?"

"Yes!" Audrey clapped her hands. "I'm trying something different for the strawberry festival in town this year. I'm thinking pretzel salad with strawberries, and I have some of those big fat pretzels for sale, too."

Violet nodded. "Neat."

As her sister and grandmother fell into the familiar rhythm of routine conversation, Ivy started to relax. She hadn't planned to be—and didn't want to be—comforted by her grandmother and her childhood home, but she was. Still, thoughts of her mother crept into her mind. Hopefully, the answers she was looking for were still there.

Audrey turned to Ivy, a gleam in her eyes. "Oh, I am just so excited to have both my girls here. Come tell me all about what we've missed." She gestured to the kitchen table. "I'll make tea."

Audrey stood on the porch, absorbing the evening weather that had just begun to turn warmer with the spring. As the neighboring farmer's tractor cut rows in the dark earth, it cast a trail of dust behind it like a smoky tail. Barn swallows followed, swooping toward the ground to catch their last meal of the day. The wind blew across the fields toward the orchards, and a silvery shimmer mixed with the dust. She folded her arms over her chest as she stared hard at the light of the fading sunset, wishing she really could see the future in the clouds, the way her mother had claimed to.

Even as a child, Audrey had feared her mother's quiet dread, and once grown, she'd refused to pass that feeling on to her own children. Lena Ashby had never really stopped believing in the old ways. Though she'd kept her rituals secret from her husband, Lena had never stopped watching the clouds.

The screen door made a hollow, wooden squeak as Ivy joined her on the porch. The young woman ducked beneath hanging baskets filled with herbs and flowers. After a moment of contemplation, Ivy nodded toward the streaks in the wind. "Someone's coming."

"Yes." Audrey reached an arm around Ivy's shoulder and pulled her granddaughter to her. "Someone is coming."

"I don't think it's good company, either," Ivy said.

The wind rustling through the trees drowned out most of the other evening noises, but the sound of the tractor's motor carried across the open fields. Audrey inhaled deeply. The new blooms on the lilac bushes that grew around the house blended nicely with the fragrance of apple blossoms and the scent of rosemary in the planters guarding the front door.

The sensation of trouble eluded Audrey, but she didn't doubt her granddaughter's intuition. "What makes you think it's not good?"

"Not sure. Just a feeling."

They stood for a moment, watching the wind whisk thin clouds across the silhouette of the sinking, swollen sun. Then Ivy patted Audrey's arm, slipped from beneath her embrace, and gave her a kiss on the cheek. After Ivy disappeared into the house, Audrey stood alone on the porch. Though almost a week had passed since Ivy moved back, Audrey's uneasy feeling lingered—and seemed to be growing. A silent, unnamed dread was creeping into her gut, but she still attributed it to having an extra person in the house. Ivy had come home for several weeks every summer, but the final move felt different because it was the end of one thing and the beginning of another. Change always unnerved Audrey. And Ivy's uncertainty was palpable—just as Rachel's had been. Audrey also couldn't ignore the eerie presence that seemed to have accompanied her granddaughter, who no doubt felt it, too. Then there was the magic in the clouds.

Maybe our visitor's already here. The thought made her shiver in the darkness. After taking one long look over the yard and the field beyond, she followed Ivy into the house, flipping on every light switch she passed.

Violet had spent most of the morning working her way through the farm's quarterly taxes, schedules, and receipts—not her favorite part of the job. With a groan, she looked up at the calendar. The idea of putting off the task for a couple of weeks was tempting. "But if I wait too close to the fifteenth and screw something up, I'm out of time to finish it."

Leaning back to stretch, she looked out the window and watched as a sheet of rain advanced toward the house. The downdrafts of the early-June storm built into a wall of clouds, pushing a small surge of dirt and newly fallen maple-tree seeds along the drive as it ushered the rain up to the house. The farm was battened down for dreary weather, leaving Violet with little to do except the long-overdue bookkeeping. It wasn't her favorite part of the job.

But somebody *has to do it.* She had hoped that Ivy would be that someone taking over once she was resettled, giving Violet more time to work with the crops and customers, but after almost a month, Ivy hadn't shown much interest. Violet had begun to wonder if her sister had any intention of working on the farm. She sighed and returned her thoughts to the task at hand.

As Violet worked, the pounding rain gave way to a gentle and gloomy mist. The phone on her desk sprang to life, startling her. A quick glance at the screen told her that Beverly was calling from the tenant house across the yard.

Cheered by the distraction from her chore, Violet answered, "Hey, Bev. What's up?"

"Violet, there's a man out by the field between our houses," Beverly said, getting right to the point. The older woman sounded calm, but Violet detected an edge of urgency to her voice.

Violet sat upright and, as Beverly continued to speak, crossed through her office and out into the dining room to look out the window toward the house where Beverly and Sam lived. Though Sam had retired over a decade ago and was no longer a farmhand for the Grants, he and Beverly were part of the family. And Sam, who spent a fair amount of time looking out the window, was a good watchdog.

"He's been there for quite a while and standing in the rain an' all. He's just kind of standing there, looking at our house." Beverly's concern was understandable. The farm hardly ever had unexpected visitors, and even expected ones were rare on a rainy day. A single guy just hanging around was certainly suspect.

Violet spotted the solitary man, short and stocky, at the edge of the field where the pumpkin patches would be planted. In the fall, she might have expected shoppers who had come to pick their own jack-o-lantern pumpkins, but not in the late spring. And at that moment, he stood motionless just on the other side of the fence that separated yard from field.

Facing the other house, he was turned slightly away from the main house, but Violet didn't think she recognized him.

"I just wanted to let you girls know in case he's up to no good," Beverly continued. "Sam's got the shotgun out, and he's fixing to go talk to him."

"How long has he been out there, Bev?" Violet was nearly breathless in her anticipation of some sort of movement, but the man continued to stand there, stock-still.

"Oh, least an hour. That's when I noticed him. I'm not much on looking outside on a dreary day like this one. So he's been there maybe longer."

An entire hour, Bev? Beverly didn't usually have much tolerance for strange events. Violet heard Beverly shift the phone.

"Are you looking outside right now? You see him?" Bev asked.

"Yes, I see him. Do you know who he is?" Realization suddenly struck Violet—she had been completely alone in the house for most of the day. Audrey and Ivy had left on a shopping trip early that morning. She glanced at the clock above the curio cabinet in the dining room. It was three o'clock. That meant she hadn't left that office for at least two hours. Violet turned slowly to look around. The house was big, and if someone had come inside, she might not have heard anything. From where she was standing, she could see that the front door's deadbolt was engaged. She leaned around the entrance to the kitchen and saw that the door there was also locked. She breathed a still-apprehensive sigh of relief.

"No, I don't know him," Beverly answered. "I just noticed it was really odd that he was standing there in the rain like that. It really can't be warm enough with just those clothes on in weather like this. And he has not moved *an inch* that I can tell."

The morning's heavy rain had washed away any warmth that might have managed to cling to the air during the unseasonably cool spring. The man had to be soaked if he'd been standing there for an hour or more. Even though the precipitation had trailed off to a fine mist, it was still enough to soak clothes and chill a person to the bone.

"How did you let a guy stand out there for an hour, Bev?" Violet asked, trying not to sound as if she were chastising her. An ache in her gut told her that something about the man was seriously wrong. He definitely hadn't come for anything from the farm store—if that had been the case, he surely would have knocked on the door of the house before waiting in the rain.

The house was far enough off the main road that anyone looking for help after a car accident or breakdown would have had to pass several homes before getting to the farm. So if he'd needed help of some kind, he would have passed up many better opportunities. *And plenty of people have cell phones nowadays.* Trekking to nearby houses for a phone was becoming a thing of the past. He also appeared to have crossed through the woods and the neighbor's field. *Maybe he banged his head in an accident, and just wandered off in a random direction.*

Beverly hadn't answered the question, and Violet heard Sam talking to Bev in the background.

"Sam says you ought to get your gun out, Violet," Bev said, returning to the phone. "'Specially if you're all alone."

Violet clutched the pendant around her neck. Her grandmother had given it to her when she was younger and told her to always wear it for protection. Symbols like the ones on Ivy's matching bracelet were etched into the back of the smooth white stone where it touched her skin. Audrey had tied several knots in the braided cord that held it. Violet had always put her faith in her grandmother's charm. *Still, not a bad idea to at least make sure the gun safe's locked.*

"Yeah, tell him that I'm going to do that now," she told Beverly, even though she had no intention of actually opening the cabinet. Neither Violet nor Ivy had been particularly interested in guns after Grandpa Jack died, so they had mostly remained in the heavy metal cabinet that rested within a wood frame clamped to the wall.

Violet's anxiousness to get to the attic, which had been Grandpa Jack's office once upon a time, chased her up the stairs quickly enough to leave her out of breath at the top. She surveyed the sparsely furnished room. Satisfied that everything—including the locked gun cabinet—was as it should have been, she peered out the window facing the other house.

The man was vacantly watching the house. *What's he looking at?* From her vantage point higher in the house, she could see that the mist was wrapping itself around him like a cocoon. *Something is definitely wrong.* Magic was starting to form, or maybe it was already fully formed, just weak. Fog couldn't hide serious magic from anyone who knew what to look for, but it had certainly fooled Beverly and Sam.

Violet felt a sudden urge to tell Beverly what was really going on. "The fog. That's why he's here in the rain—"

"What?" Beverly asked, her voice far away from the phone as if she'd been speaking to Sam. Her voice was louder when she added, "Sam's going to go out and try to talk to him."

"No!" Violet hissed. "Don't do that. Just… ummm… I think we should call the county cops."

The air around the man seemed to waver, like the heat coming off hot metal on a sunny summer day. A faint buzz of electricity tingled the hairs on Violet's arms.

"They'll be a while getting here, if they come," Beverly said. She and Sam were pretty ardent believers in enforcing the law themselves. So was Audrey. Growing up in the country where the "local" police were miles away had made them pretty independent when it came to self-defense.

"He's already been there an hour. If he was really all that dangerous, he would have done something. I'm going to at least call so they can be on the way if Sam goes out there." Violet pushed an air of authority into her tone. She wasn't sure what sort of danger the strange man posed to an old man with a shotgun—or if that shotgun posed any danger to *him*. "Hell, maybe this guy has a habit of just hanging around other people's houses. Maybe he's—"

A rustling sound on the other end of the line interrupted her. At that moment, Sam emerged through the screen door at the back of the house. He carried the shotgun pointed at the ground alongside him. When Bev started to follow him, he turned back to her, his expression stern, ready to argue.

"Oh, hell!" Violet disconnected the call. She bolted down the stairs—which seemed suddenly endless—to the first floor. She struggled with the lock on the back door, fumbling in her hurry, then banged through the screen door. Just as Sam stepped off his own porch, one arm held behind him to push Beverly back, Violet started out into the yard.

The staring man's gaze jerked toward Violet. She remembered the phone in her hand—and her intention to call the police. At the same time, a clap of thunder rattled the windows of the house behind her. Dropping the phone, Violet covered her ears with her hands. A solid wave of air and sound propelled by the silvery fog lifted her off her feet and threw her backward, flat on the ground. Sam and Beverly were a tangle of limbs—and shotgun, which Violet hoped hadn't gone off—on the porch.

The staring man took off running across the yard and down the drive toward Oak Hill, moving awkwardly, as if he'd forgotten how to use his limbs properly. In a flash, Beverly was on her feet, apparently no worse for the wear. Violet leapt to her own feet and shook her head, her ears ringing.

"What the hell was that?" Sam shouted, but Violet could hardly hear him.

Beverly snatched the gun from him and crouched beside him, prodding at his clothes.

"I'm fine, Bev!" He pulled away, straightening his clothes. "Where did he go?"

"That way." Violet turned to point in the direction in which the man had fled. Her voice trailed off as she realized she'd let him out of her sight. Before Sam could charge after the fleeing man—and get himself into trouble—Violet sprinted toward the orchard, hoping to catch him first.

A second earlier, the man had seemed headed toward town, but he wasn't visible in the open field, so he must have turned in toward the orchard. As she ran across the open spaces that occupied the property, it occurred to her just how very strange it was that he had been standing in the wide open when he could have at least somewhat concealed himself among the trees that grew close to both houses. *Gran was worried about a visitor...*

She raced through the rows of trees until she realized she had no idea what she would do if she did find him. He had looked too big for her to overpower physically, and she wasn't carrying anything to protect herself. *Oh, shit—the phone!* Despite Violet's height advantage, if he jumped out and grabbed her, she would probably go down. He'd also been working magic she'd never seen before. He'd obviously been up to something, and she still wasn't certain what kind of danger he posed.

Completely out of breath, she stopped running. *I can't be that out of shape!* If that short, stout man was still running, and still moving that fast, then he had to be in very good shape. Violet turned to see Beverly and Sam in pursuit of her. Sam still had his gun, and Beverly had taken up a long bamboo stake she must have pulled from the edge of Audrey's garden, prepared to protect Violet with whatever was at hand.

Sam was armed and ready, on alert, his eyes roving over everything. "He doesn't look to be coming back soon," he said, prowling the trees like an angry bear, acting every inch the protective male, a role he'd taken up after Jack passed away.

"Well, we are definitely going to call the police and report this." Violet motioned Sam and Bev back to the house. "Come on. I'll make us tea."

Chapter Four

AUDREY PULLED UP TO HER house to find a police car in the drive. She was sure right away that it had something to do with the unsettling feeling she hadn't been able to shake off lately. Still, since nothing else appeared to be amiss, Audrey doubted anything too terrible was happening. And Violet *had* become fairly friendly with one of the younger police officers in town. *But he's never been to visit the house, let alone driven up in a police car.*

"Oh my God. What's this about?" Ivy sprang out of the car like a jackrabbit even before Audrey had put the car in park.

"I'm sure it's fine," Audrey called after her, hustling to catch up. The residue of foreign magic prickled her skin. But she hurried to the house, making a mental note to think about whose magic it was at a later time.

"Well, it sounded so strange, and I didn't think it would hurt to just drop by since I was already in the area," a man's voice was saying as Ivy burst into the house just ahead of Audrey.

"What—" Ivy stopped at the door, her mouth half open.

Audrey gave a gentle push, forcing Ivy to move farther into the room, where everyone stared calmly at her after her blustery entrance.

"What's going on?" Ivy finished quietly.

Officer Kevin Bonniere was at the table with Violet, Sam, and Beverly, scribbling notes into a steno pad.

Sam turned to face them. "Some odd man in the pumpkin patch, Aud. Violet thought we ought to bother the police." With a patronizing look on his face, he jerked his head in the girl's direction. "I had my gun out already."

The young officer shrugged. "Well, it wasn't any trouble—aside from your own, sir." He stood and offered Audrey his outstretched hand. "Officer Bonniere, ma'am. I got a call from your granddaughter about a guy standing in the rain in your yard. He took off, and I didn't see anything of him when I drove up. These three didn't seem to think he was dangerous, so just keep an eye out for him. Give us a call if he shows up again."

Audrey shook his hand with one strong pump of her elbow. Taking in the man's broad shoulders and kind eyes, Audrey could see why her granddaughter liked him. "Well, thank you for coming, young man. We appreciate it." She shot Sam a frown.

He nodded to Ivy. "Ma'am."

Standing next to the door, Ivy screwed up her face a little and gave him a short wave.

Officer Bonniere looked down at this notepad and flipped a couple of pages in what was obviously an attempt to make a graceful exit. "Well, I think I've got everything I need here. You let me know if you need anything else." He directed his words at Sam and Beverly. Then his eyes briefly met Violet's, and a pale-pink blush painted the tips of his ears.

"Here, I'll point out where he was standing and which way he went, just for your notes." Violet rose from her seat almost slowly enough for her nonchalance to be convincing.

Audrey caught the glimmer in the young man's eye.

"All right. Lead the way," he said, sweeping an arm toward the door.

As Violet led Officer Bonniere outside, Audrey turned back to Sam and Bev. "So unfriendly visitors, huh?"

Frowning, Sam shook his head. "Just standing out there in the rain like some kind of nut."

"But when Sam went out there…" Bev clapped her hands above her head. "Bang! Something knocked him clean on his hind end."

Audrey frowned and raised an eyebrow. She looked out the window at the yard, thinking of the magic she'd sensed. *It wasn't ours.*

"I guess our visitor's arrived," Ivy said, drawing everyone's attention. "The silver on the wind…" She gestured vaguely toward the window.

"Must be." Audrey nodded solemnly.

Chapter Five

"MIGHT AS WELL UNPACK IT all." Ivy flopped the decades-old suitcase onto the bed. It was full of her winter clothes, which she'd left in the suitcase for the last few weeks, simply because she hadn't needed them.

Ivy ran her hands over the front of the case, thinking of her mother. The suitcase had belonged to Rachel Grant, who had taken it with her the day she'd left home for the first time. But she'd left it behind when she left for good. The faded luggage was a tenuous connection to a part of Ivy's own past that she would never recall. She'd always wondered if Rachel had packed it with baby clothes and taken it with her to the hospital in Georgia, where Ivy and Violet were born.

When she'd finished putting her clothes away, she pulled a book from the suitcase pocket and laid it on the bed. The Book of Shadows was her personal log of the magic she'd learned from her grandmother as well as Wiccan friends. Most of the spells she'd collected were intended to find lost people—but none had led to her mother. Even the trip that Ivy and her friend Rhiannon had made to the hospital listed on her birth certificate had led to a dead end.

She sighed, staring at the only remaining occupant of the suitcase: a small lacquered pine box. Ivy flipped the silver clasp to reveal an athame nestled on a purple velvet pillow, its white opal blade whetted to a fine edge.

The box was a present from Rhiannon, but Ivy had found the dagger behind the lining of her mother's old suitcase. Ivy gripped the silver handle, wondering what her mother had used it for—and why she'd left it hidden in the raggedy luggage. *For me to find? For Violet?*

She and Rhiannon had discussed it many times. Ivy felt a twinge of sadness at having left her friend behind. But then a smile tugged at her lips as she thought of the first time she'd seen Rhiannon, during her first semester of college.

Ivy had stumbled upon Bewitching Word during an afternoon walk. Carrying a Starbuck's cup in one hand and a drenched umbrella in the other, she'd ducked under the awning to avoid the downpour that had begun as a slight drizzle.

"Hello, dear. Why don't you come inside and wait for this to pass?"

Ivy turned to find a curvy young woman holding open the door of the shop, beckoning her inside. The woman's wide, genuine smile reached all the way to her brown-gold eyes.

"Sure. Thank you," Ivy answered, grateful for the reprieve from the weather and drawn to the positive vibe that radiated from the woman.

"Crazy weather, huh? It's the 'lake effects' or some such nonsense." The woman's long purple broom skirt swished behind her as she walked inside. She led Ivy to a small table with two mismatched chairs.

Looking around, Ivy realized she was surrounded by shelves full of books about witchcraft, Wicca, and spell work. The shop sold bells, cauldrons, crystals, and—

"Wands!" Ivy whispered. Her grandmother had never used one, but Ivy had read about them.

Rhiannon had clapped her hands happily. "Oh, I just knew you belonged here the moment I saw you." For hours, they'd talked about magic and mothers while sipping tea.

With a sigh of regret, Ivy returned the knife to its box and clicked the clasp into place. After tucking the box and the Book of Shadows back into the suitcase, she zipped the case closed and stowed it under her bed with the rest of her luggage. Though Violet wanted nothing to do with discussing their mother, Ivy was determined to solve the mystery. *She left behind too many clues to not want us to find her.* Violet was outside, working in the orchard, which gave Ivy the perfect opportunity to do a little uninterrupted searching. Armed with fresh magical insight, she was certain that the same old items she'd seen before held new information now that she had a better understanding of what to look for. Rachel had certainly known about her own magic—and that knowledge had somehow taken her away from her mother and children.

In the sitting room, Ivy looked over her shoulder despite knowing she was alone. Her grandmother wouldn't mind that she was looking through the albums, but Ivy wasn't keen on having another argument with Violet about her interest in their mother. The farmhouse held few physical reminders of Ivy's mother—her grandmother and grandpa seemed to have turned all their focus to their granddaughters once they realized Rachel was not coming back.

The lack of memorabilia on display never seemed intentional, especially since albums that held plenty of pictures of Rachel Grant sat right alongside others on the shelf in the sitting room. Ivy had seen the pictures maybe a hundred times. Still, she harbored a delicate hope that they would lead her to some lost connection with her mother.

She pulled a familiar dusty, leather-bound album from the shelf and opened it to the first page. The black-and-white photo of a petite young woman standing in front of a train car, flanked by two muscular men wearing tight clothing, had always been her favorite. A heavy woven sweater covered the woman's dress, which was made of many overlapping layers of thin fabric. A dark braid encircled her head like a wreath.

"Ken, Lena, Pat" was scrawled beneath the photo. When she was young, Ivy's great-grandmother had traveled with a carnival, telling fortunes and doing magic tricks. But she didn't care for the carnival life, so she'd saved her coins and followed the good luck to America, where she'd met a lovely young man.

Ivy smiled and touched a finger gently to the picture. Below, the same woman, dressed in a traditional white wedding gown, stood beside a young man in a suit. Printed carefully along the bottom of the photo was "Kenneth and Lena Ashby on their wedding day."

Ivy recalled her thirteenth birthday, the first time her grandmother had shown her the photos. "My mother was special, and so was your mother. And so are you," Audrey had told Ivy and Violet. "I sometimes forget that I won't be here for you forever. You need to know that we are different because it will help you protect yourselves, and each other, if I'm not there."

As Ivy remembered her grandmother's words, she cast another glance over her shoulder to make sure she was still alone then pulled out the two albums she was looking for. Something shifted and slipped down behind them as if it had been carelessly left on the top of the stack. Sliding the other albums aside, she found a box she'd never seen before. A peek below the lid revealed a collection of unsorted photos—fresh clues! She set the box on top of the photo albums and took the pile to her room. Among the familiar faces of relatives and family friends in the assorted pictures, she found one that she'd noticed before but couldn't put a name to. The man appeared in a few of the photographs in the albums as well.

Tucking several loose photos into the book, Ivy went in search of her grandmother. "Hey, Gran?" she called out as she took the stairs to the attic, photo album in hand.

"Sure, dear." Audrey stood at the arched window, holding a coffee mug full of tea.

"Who is this?" Ivy held the book open to a page with a picture of Grandpa Jack and a young man standing together, each proudly holding a big fish. "I was sorting your box of photos." Balancing the book in one hand, she placed the loose Polaroids next to the photo.

"Are you that bored?" Audrey asked with a smile. "Gave up on the job postings already?"

Ivy cringed inwardly. She hadn't realized her grandmother had seen her looking through the want ads in the newspaper. "Um, yeah, I guess so," she said quietly. She looked out the window, avoiding her grandmother's gaze, but the orchard had already consumed Audrey's attention. Irritated, Ivy leaned forward to get a better view of what was so important.

Outside, Violet walked the path through the grove of apple trees, hanging mason jars from the branches. Entranced, Ivy watched her sister from the attic window as the storm rumbled closer and the clouds grew darker. The wind teased Violet's dark hair, lifting it from her shoulders. Thick, heavy drops of rain began to plop into the dry dirt around her.

A few drops smacked the window in front of Audrey and Ivy. Then the rain started in earnest, and lightning crackled across the sky with fierce intensity. The static electricity caught Violet's fluttering hair, and strands waved around her face as if they were tentacles floating in water. Ivy jumped as a bolt of lightning streaked through the sky toward the ground. The trees seemed to gather the electricity and pass the glow on to the woman standing in their midst. Silvery sparks rained from the trees, hitting a shimmering globe that surrounded Violet. The light shrank closer to her body until it appeared to melt into her.

"What's she doing?" Ivy asked her grandmother.

"Rainwater collected during a lightning storm has more energy," Audrey answered, gesturing to the jars hung in the trees, apparently unfazed by the events unfolding in the orchard. "That's what the jars are for. She's been extra concerned since she saw the strange man in the field."

Ivy didn't blame her sister for being worried. Even though three days had passed, traces of the unsettling magic still lingered in the air like an oily sheen on water. But that business in the orchard was unusual, even for her family.

Ivy looked at her grandmother with a raised eyebrow. "How's she doing that with the orb?"

Audrey shrugged, looking away from the window and toward Ivy. "I'm not sure she knows it's there. I think it just happens."

"Fascinating," Ivy said quietly as they both watched out the window. She smiled, thinking of the electric static that always seemed to accompany Violet's nervousness. Though Audrey had taught Violet and Ivy to read the nature around them, Violet had clearly matured into a natural magic that was very different from the magic in Ivy, who drew her power from learning about magic. Ivy felt a spark when she found new knowledge in a book or learned a spell from another person. Her magic felt connected more to a shared past… a part of which was missing. She frowned at the open book still in her hands, stifling a sigh.

With a sigh of her own, Audrey set her tea on the window ledge and took the book, peering at the picture tucked into the binding. "Oh, I forget his name. Mike? Or Mark? I don't remember." Holding the page with her thumb, she flipped the book closed to look at the cover then opened it again. "So much has happened since then. He dated your mother for a while in high school. Grandpa Jack liked him a lot." A grin spread across her face. "Look how handsome Grandpa is!" She laughed a little, making Ivy smile. "Don't remember whatever happened to the boy, though. I think he lives in town, real estate agent or something, maybe?" She shrugged.

Despite Audrey's nonchalant attitude, Ivy's heart caught every time someone spoke of her mother. She wondered if her grandmother was secretly holding on to the same curiosity that filled Ivy. She tried to close the door on the thought, but it slipped in anyway. *Could that boy be my father?* The next few thoughts snuck in through the cracks. *Did he have kids? Do I have more brothers or sisters right next door?*

Ivy stared at one of the photos. In it, her mother was wearing a loose red top and bell-bottoms, her long hair pulled back into a neat braid. Instead of looking into the camera, Rachel smiled warmly at a cat snuggled in her arms. The year—1980—was handwritten beneath the Polaroid. Rachel was fifteen. She looked happy. *Was she?* Ivy knew that two years after that photo was taken, Rachel left home with nothing but a suitcase. Two years after that, she came home with two newborns in tow and little else. When she went away the second time, Rachel left everything behind. More remembered words from her grandmother floated to the surface of Ivy's mind: "I want you to know that she didn't leave because of you. It was because of me. I made a mistake by not telling her who we are. She shouldn't have had to go looking for answers."

The memory faded as Ivy's eyes drifted to the boy in the picture. She knew he wasn't her father—the years didn't add up—but logic had always failed to keep the question at bay. Though Ivy had a birth certificate, it didn't list her father's name. A knot formed in her stomach.

She realized that she and Audrey had both been staring quietly at the photos for quite a while. When she looked up, her grandmother slowly met her gaze, offering her a wan smile.

"Sorry, kiddo," she whispered. "I wish I knew, too. I put so many pictures in albums, not knowing they were going to hurt later."

Ivy blinked hard and swallowed her tears. "I know. It's okay."

Thunder rattled the windows, and Audrey collected her teacup from the ledge then put an arm around Ivy's shoulders. "Let's go see if we can't find something better to reminisce about."

Ivy slipped the photo album onto a shelf, next to a few other books, before they went downstairs.

Violet walked between the trees, listening to the thunder tumble across the sky. The lightning snapped and crackled through the atmosphere then rolled over her, promising a lively storm. She took a deep breath, inhaling the smell of the rain.

She pulled another empty Mason jar from the wooden crate. Holding the cotton cord tied tightly around the wide mouth, she looked for the sturdiest branch. They had been pruned so that only the best branches remained—they weren't shade trees, after all—but some of the boughs still needed training. She found one that pointed skyward then carefully tucked the leaves through the loop as she threaded the branch through. When she let go of the jar, the branch didn't droop at all. She nodded, happy with her choice.

The faint trace of magic that the strange lurking man had left behind lingered longer than it should have. Violet hoped the storm would cleanse the air around the house. The charged rainwater would give her and Audrey more water they could work magic on then sprinkle around the house and maybe give a little boost to a few of the plants.

As she hung the next jar, she threw a glance over her shoulder at the drive, still a little unsettled by how easily the man had crept up on the house and how quickly he'd disappeared. She thought of Kevin and how she would explain herself if he showed up just then. *Oh, just hoping for some magic rain. That's not strange at all.* She wondered if he'd heard the rumors already or the gossip about her mother. That was bound to happen sooner or later. She'd heard a few stories about him—or his parents, at least—so she had no doubt the rumor mill was churning.

A streak of lightning told her she needed to finish up fast. Even for her, hanging out under a tree during a lightning storm wasn't a good idea. She hung the last of the jars, being less particular about the placement than she'd been at the beginning. Then she headed back to the house, shivering in the slight chill that had accompanied the first few drops of rain.

She was just under the cover of the porch roof when the rain started to fall in earnest. Violet deposited the empty crate next to the steps, alongside trespassing morning glory vines creeping up the foundation, and stood, watching the rain. Something brushed her leg, making her jump. Tom Cat looked up at her expectantly.

"Sorry, Tom. No can do," she said, kneeling beside him to ruffle his yellow fur. "You know you have no business coming into the house. You should have hightailed it to the shed before it started."

He meowed at her, giving her a sullen sideways glance, and leapt up to his usual perch on the windowsill. He wobbled a little then settled down into the planter, which they no longer bothered to plant since he'd claimed it as his personal spot. She rolled her eyes at the clumsy cat before turning back to the yard. The stranger had been standing watch during the rain the last time, but that hadn't been a full-fledged storm. Still, she wondered if he might return during the storm, with the mist as his cover. That would give her an excuse to call Kevin at least. *Just call him anyway, you chicken,* she thought. "We should get chickens," she said aloud to no one in particular, changing the subject of the conversation she was having with herself.

Tom Cat meowed as if in answer.

"Yep, you'd probably just eat 'em. I know." With a groan, she opened the screen door. She could practically hear her grandmother's voice in her head: *"Just go call the boy, Violet."*

Feeling especially like a chicken at that moment, she locked the door behind her and peeked outside once more. She couldn't quite shake the sensation of someone nearby watching—or the thought that she wasn't the one being watched. *This sort of thing never happens when Ivy's not home.* Shivers crept up her spine and across her scalp.

Chapter Six

IVY LOOKED AT HER SISTER as they sat in the grass in the front yard. The sun reflected off her long dark hair, reminding Ivy of the sun glinting off the wings of a blackbird. Violet was tan in that unintentional way of people who lived their lives outside. She seemed so at home and so happy on the farm.

Stroking the fat yellow tomcat that had settled next to her, Ivy looked out across the fields and the leafy green boscage whose farthest edge disappeared over the smooth, subtle hills. "It's funny how being away for even a little while makes you feel strange when you get back."

"I wouldn't know. I've never really been anywhere." Her eyes closed against the bright sun, Violet smiled almost as if she were teasing, but Ivy wasn't sure.

"Everything here reminds me of when we were little—places we played and things like that. When we chased bugs or waited for the tadpoles to turn into baby frogs…" Ivy ran her fingers through the cat's fur, shaking away loose hairs. "And the sky's so big here… and the trees. Hell, even the house is big. It makes me remember being little, and even though I know I'm not anymore, it makes me feel small and faraway but still like everything is too close."

"When you go away, you're surrounded by people who don't know you, and it's kind of like you're free and faraway, no matter how close they are," Violet said.

"Yeah, that's exactly what it's like." Ivy was amazed to think that her sister, who always seemed to know right where she belonged, might feel the same as she did. But Violet was just fine—she belonged right where she already was. Ivy had spent her whole life waiting to fit in, hoping that growing up would make her a part of something. She wasn't comfortable in her own skin in Oak Hill—or anywhere, really. Everyone seemed to know she was different.

Watching Violet from the corner of her eye, Ivy felt more distant from her own sister than she did from anyone else. Violet had been cut from the most beautiful cloth that they made in Marshall County. Ivy looked at her own hands and fingers then at her sister's. Ivy had spent a great deal of time looking at other people's hands. She and her sister had the same hands, with long delicate fingers extended from square-shaped palms. They seemed to share that trait with no one else in their family. She wondered whose hands those were.

She thought of the photographs of their mother, none of which really showed her hands. She wondered if her hands were like her mother's. *Perhaps they're our father's hands…*

In the country, everyone knew everyone else's secrets. But Rachel Grant had managed to keep one desperate secret from everyone in her hometown… including her own mother and daughters. "Do you ever wonder if Mom—"

Violet jumped to her feet and dusted dirt and loose grass from her hands and the backs of her legs. "Look, I *know* there's a whole world out there, but I don't need it. That's just not me. I know you're different." She shrugged as if shaking off a bad feeling. "If you don't want to stay, you don't have to." She sounded a bit harsher than Ivy suspected she'd intended to. "I think maybe you like it here, and you like feeling small and remembering running through the grass and baby frogs and all that. You just don't want to like it because all anyone ever says is that they want to grow up and get out of here. It's not about those other people, though. You do whatever *you* want to do."

Ivy squinted up at her sister. Violet apparently understood how she was feeling, though she did not share Ivy's concerns for the future. Violet shrugged again then turned toward the trees, leaving Ivy to ruminate. Then even the fat cat abandoned her to stroll off after Violet.

"Well, I see where I stand around here," she told the cat, who gave her a deadpan glance over his shoulder.

Ivy knew she could stay on the farm and help Violet run it. Her sister was actually running a pretty big business all on her own. A significant portion of that business involved renting out much of their land to other farmers, and Ivy had, after all, studied business in college. And the Internet offered lots of new opportunities she knew Violet hadn't thought of. But all of that meant staying in Marshall County, where nothing seemed to happen. *But where else would I go?* She could stay with her friend Rhiannon, but that would mean returning to the city, and she wasn't sure she liked that any more than she liked Marshall County. Unable to come up with a better answer, she turned to stare at the house. *I guess I have my answer—for now. Until I find my mother.*

"Oh, hell," she muttered. Then she stood and went inside in search of distractions.

Ivy didn't sleep well that night. An innominate, shadowy figure had begun to haunt the corners of her dreams and the edges of her imagination over the last several weeks. It had wended its way into her nightmares after her roommate had moved out of the apartment. She had attributed it to the anxiety of being a young woman living alone in the city. But her roommate had spent most of her time at her boyfriend's house anyway, so Ivy wasn't that much more alone after the move than she had been beforehand. And then the manifestation had followed Ivy back to the countryside, carrying along with it a singular desire to control her sleeping thoughts. Lately, it threatened to punch through the barrier between sleeping and waking as she found herself uncomfortable in the darkness more and more often.

So she rose with the birds at the very first light of the morning. Ivy was dressed and outside, looking over Audrey's garden before the other women were stirring. Audrey always planted during the proper moon cycle and laid her seeds out on the night of the first full moon of spring to soak in the moonlight.

The dew still clung to the grass, soaking her sneakers as she walked. Early mornings weren't something that she partook of often, but she found them enjoyable. The sun always seemed to sparkle more as it cast soft shadows through the trees.

She had forgotten how much she missed just being with the flowers and herbs that grew in her grandmother's garden each summer. She bent, smelling the mint and lavender. Two chickadees argued fiercely in the yard. Sudden disappointment washed over Ivy: she had already missed the crocuses and tulips, which had bloomed earlier in the year.

She crossed to the patch where her grandmother grew strawberries for the locally famous pies and tarts that she sold at the markets and in the store. Before long, Audrey and Bev, along with a hired hand or two, would be spending a great deal of time harvesting the plump red berries. *A week or two.* She noted the number of small green berries that had already formed. Marigolds had recently been planted in the bare spots throughout the garden to keep the aphids away.

Thoughts of her cryptic dreamtime companion dissipated in the crisp light of the morning sun. She sat on the small wooden bench at the edge of the patch and closed her eyes, letting the rising sun wash over her face, filling her with warmth. The screen door of the house squeaked open then closed with a light slap. Ivy squinted toward the house to see her grandmother coming over, holding two coffee mugs with steam rising from their rims. Audrey was wearing a long denim shirt over cropped, fraying white jeans.

"I brought you some tea." She sat next to Ivy and offered her one of the cups.

Ivy thanked her and took it, careful not to spill the contents. She sipped gingerly at the hot liquid. Ivy had never really shared her grandmother's ability to drink scalding beverages without so much as a wince. As usual, the tea was far too hot for Ivy's preference.

Audrey surveyed the expansive garden as she drank her own tea.

"It looks good, Gran."

"Yes, it does." Audrey nodded. "The weather seems to get warmer earlier every year." For a moment, she was silent, looking at Ivy through the corner of her eye. "What are you doing up so early?" she asked finally.

"I just couldn't sleep. I start thinking about things, and I just can't get back to sleep." She stared intently into the cup, not certain she was ready to tell her grandmother about the strange dreams and the deep foreboding that insisted something bad had followed her to the farm. She thought of the tarot card reading Rhiannon had done for her, but she didn't know for sure how her grandmother would react. Audrey didn't seem to know about that sort of magic, or maybe she just didn't believe in it.

"You probably just aren't used to the house again," Audrey said.

"I've been feeling kind of bad since before graduation," Ivy told her. "Just jittery, like I'm waiting for something to happen, but I don't know what." She looked around at the house and yard.

Audrey followed her gaze.

"Sometimes, I feel like I'm not sure I made any of the right decisions about things. I don't know if I belong here, Gran."

"Well, you know I'd do anything for you, but you won't be happy with it if I make those decisions for you."

"I know," Ivy said quietly. "Sometimes, I wish it was that easy, though... if you could just decide for me." Ivy offered her a feeble smile that she knew didn't touch her face beyond her lips. It wouldn't have mattered if it had. Even though Audrey might have been losing her ability to read her granddaughter, she still knew Ivy well enough to see her expression for what it was.

Audrey smiled a weak smile of her own and patted Ivy's knee. "I would be very happy if you stayed, but not if it is going to make you miserable. There's no point in that."

"I don't know where else I would go," Ivy said quietly. Her fingers hugged her mug so tightly that the tips of her fingers turned dark pink. "I can't seem to find my place." Her feelings of uncertainty were still close to the surface, so she let them spill over. Those were the normal sorts of fears, ones she could share.

"Well, life has a way of leading us where we should go. Just do what you feel is best, and you'll find your place. I would imagine it's hard out there on your own, but people do it every day." A heavy breath escaped Gran's lips. "I wouldn't want to do it, but my mother did it. She was so much stronger than me, though. Sometimes I think of the things she did to get by, and I'm amazed." She shook her head slowly, as if pondering her mother's past or perhaps her own ability to compromise.

A tentative silence settled over Ivy and her grandmother as they sat in the garden, watching the sun creep higher into the eastern sky.

"Hel-lo!" Bev called from across the yard as she waved. She was making her way over to them with her own mug in hand.

Wanting to avoid having Beverly see her cry, Ivy made an excuse about needing to finish something for Violet and left with a short, half-hearted wave.

"She was in an awful hurry. Hope it wasn't something I said," Beverly joked as she sat in the now-empty spot on the bench. The playfulness slipped from her face when she turned to look at Audrey, who hadn't succeeded in keeping the pensive look from her eyes. "What's wrong, dear?"

Audrey shook her head. "I just don't know about that girl... sometimes she's so much like her mother, secretive and wild-eyed, like she's looking for something I can't give her. I'm scared she's going to go looking for something she has to give herself."

"Oh, don't worry, Aud. She won't go off like Rachel did. It's a different day and age, anyway."

They watched Ivy dart up the porch steps and into the house.

"It isn't easy to just disappear like it used to be. Computers and cell phones. The Internet and all that..." Beverly waved her hand in a vague gesture. "I don't know anything about all that stuff, but people do." She shrugged and smiled.

"I don't know if I could do it again, not knowing." Rachel had called Audrey one afternoon from the diner where she worked as a waitress after school. She'd told her mother she was going away to visit a friend for the weekend. At eighteen, Rachel was responsible beyond her years, so Audrey hadn't questioned it. Then the weekend turned into weeks, and a few postcards trickled in before Audrey lost touch with her for almost two years.

"You did so many things differently this time—even if Ivy left, she wouldn't just disappear." Beverly nudged Audrey with her shoulder, making Audrey's coffee wiggle perilously close to the lip of the cup.

"I hope she won't."

"Now, you and I both know these girls are different. We're all of us going to be just fine." She slapped the bench board next to her thigh.

Beverly and Sam, who had never had children of their own, had always seemed content to dote on children of family and friends, especially Jack and Audrey's. Though Audrey wondered if children had simply not been in the cards for them or if they had made the choice not to have them, she'd never asked. Despite being bound to Beverly by proximity, work, and friendship, Audrey had never been certain the binds were tight enough for her to bring up the subject. And Beverly had never offered.

Beverly's encouraging smile reached her eyes, but they didn't sparkle as they usually did. The sadness that crept into that smile just before Beverly shrugged and looked away made Audrey suddenly wonder if her dearest friend might, in fact, know what it meant to lose a child. Perhaps she even felt the void left by Rachel just as strongly as Audrey did.

"Maybe we could look for her," Beverly offered quietly. "You know, hire someone. People do that, don't they?"

Audrey nodded slowly. "Maybe that's the sort of task I should set Ivy to. She knows more about those things than we do, and maybe that would satisfy her need to go looking." She nodded more vigorously. "I might check into that."

Beverly stared out at the field for a somber moment then turned back to Audrey, her brow scrunched. "Why *do* you think she left, Aud? Did… did something happen?"

Curious why Beverly had never asked before, Audrey sighed heavily. She knew that everyone must wonder that same thing. The change in the air seemed to be affecting everyone lately. A feeling in her gut told Audrey that she wouldn't get by with secrets and half-truths much longer, especially not with Beverly, not after so many years.

"No, I don't think so." She rubbed her hands together. "When she came back and brought the girls with her, I hoped that she would stay with us, Jack and me, and be a family again." She looked down at her clenched hands. "I knew in my heart that she wouldn't stay, but I never let myself admit it. I knew she needed me, but I didn't know how to help. So I told myself she was okay. And she slipped away again… but you're right. I did lots of things differently with Ivy and Violet."

Beverly and Sam almost certainly knew that Audrey and her girls were different. Audrey and Jack had never hid it, but after thousands of cups of coffee, a million cups of tea at the kitchen table, and enough laughter and tears to fill all those cups, Audrey had never explained her family to Beverly. *She knows, though. She has to know.*

So Audrey took that moment to open up and tell the story. The people in her family were different. They had once belonged to the land, near the mountains, bound by the moon and the wind and everything that dragged across the sky. More and more visitors came to the mountain villages. Then they began to stay. People would come to tell the villagers their secrets and ask for favors or love spells, but they were afraid. Eventually, the villagers who continued to believe in the old ways became outcasts in their own home. So, some of them took to traveling, looking for a new home.

"They say that the traveling became part of their nature. The magic pulled and pushed them all over. Some of us still feel that need to move, to always be moving. The ones who didn't feel the pull followed the others because they wanted to stay with their kin." She swallowed and took a deep breath, willing the sadness away from her eyes and back into her heart, where she still kept everything that belonged to her daughter. "Rachel never knew."

"Did Jack?" Beverly asked quietly.

Audrey smiled at the thought of Jack. "Yes, he knew. My mother never told my father, though. Mother told me about the past and showed me the magic. She was always afraid people would find out, that they would know she wasn't quite like them. She always felt empty without it, though—that's why she taught me. When Rachel was born, I was scared of the same thing, so I never told her. I think she took to traveling for the same reason our people did a long time ago—she was looking for a place to fit in. I never told her, like I did the girls. She never knew where we came from. Never knew how to understand that feeling." Guilt swirled in Audrey's stomach as she remembered her failure to connect with her only child.

"She was one of the 'movers' then." Beverly nodded slowly.

"I think so. I don't know that feeling myself. I know Violet doesn't have it. But Ivy… I don't know if she's just unsettled or if she's taken to wandering."

Beverly chewed at the corner of her mouth, seeming to consider that for a moment. "You know I love her like my own, but that girl's never been satisfied with a thing in her life. I don't think she really wants to leave, but she wishes she did. She wants to be a 'mover,' but she's not."

Beverly's insight was dead-on. Audrey's lips rose at the corners. "I suspect you're right. She never seemed settled in the city, and she doesn't even talk about it now."

"She's not leaving, not for good."

"If she needs to, I hope she does. But if that happens, she better damn well call once in a while."

Beverly snickered and leaned over to put her arm around Audrey's shoulder. "She would."

Chapter Seven

IVY HELD THE POLAROID NEXT to the photograph in the newspaper. The man was definitely the boy in the picture. "So Mark What's-His-Name *is* a real estate agent." She'd seen his picture in the newspaper while she was looking through the job listing, and the ad with the photograph had caught her eye immediately. Her mother's high school boyfriend was looking for an assistant. She knew the dates didn't add up—he couldn't be her father. Rachel had left town long before Ivy and Violet were born. Still, Ivy couldn't get the boy out of her head. Even if he wasn't her father, maybe he knew why Rachel had left the first time. Maybe he knew why she hadn't stayed when she'd returned.

Staring at her cell phone, Ivy sighed. She hated talking on the phone and talking to strangers. She sometimes hated talking to anybody at all. "I can't be a real estate agent." A train wreck of thoughts jumbled her head. "I like houses. Maybe I *could* be a real estate agent. I could sell a house." Before she could convince herself otherwise, she snatched up the phone and dialed Mark Morrison's phone number.

"Hiya! Morrison Realty," a sprightly female voice answered. "How can I help you?"

That was not at all what Ivy had expected. "Um, hi. I'm calling about the job ad…"

"Oh, sure. I'm Karen, Mark's secretary—and his sister." She chuckled. "Do you have a résumé?" Papers shuffled in the background. "Actually, dear—I'm sorry, I didn't get your name."

Hesitating, wondering if Karen would recognize her last name, she finally stammered, "Ivy, uh, Ivy Grant?" She shook her head, annoyed with herself and certain she sounded like an idiot who didn't even know her own name. *Uuuuugh.* "Um, yes, I have a résumé."

"Okay, Ivy, I'll tell you what—if you're interested, he's got a cancellation in about two hours, so if you want to fill that meeting, you can come on in and talk to him in person. Bring your résumé with you."

She hadn't planned to go to an interview. She hadn't really planned on… well, she didn't know what she'd been thinking when she picked up that phone. *Nothing, I suppose.* She started to shirk the unanticipated rush of opportunity. "Okay… bu—"

"Great! I've got you down for eleven o'clock. Just come to the office. I'll let him know you're coming." After a cheerful but rushed goodbye, Karen ended the call without waiting for Ivy to answer.

Fidgeting with the stone on the cord around her wrist, she chewed her lip. Excitement bubbled up inside her chest at the thought of meeting someone with such a strong connection to her mother. In the pit of her stomach, she suspected it might be the closest she would ever get to Rachel Grant.

"Crap!" She looked down at her workout clothes, which doubled as pajamas lately. *Better get dressed. Now, what do you wear to an interview for a job you don't want?*

After choosing what she thought was an appropriate interview outfit— khakis and a blue blouse—she stopped in the kitchen to write Audrey a note. With the pen still in her hand, her eyes fell to the cord bracelet. It didn't really fit the rest of her outfit. But she hadn't taken it off in years. *What could possibly happen to you at a job interview in Oak Hill?* She slipped the bracelet off and set it on the counter where she would be sure to find it when she got back. In place of the bracelet, she hummed a short protection spell of her own and drew a symbol in the air with her finger. Satisfied with her fashion compromise, Ivy flitted out the door.

Settling into the car, she shook as much of the tension out of her neck as she could. Then, with a groan, she turned the key. As she pulled out of the driveway, Ivy cranked the volume on the radio to drown out the nervous chatter in her head. Still, by the time she parked outside Morrison Realty, right off the town square, she had practiced introducing herself about two dozen times.

She took a few deep breaths, steeling herself for the meeting. "You don't even want the job. It doesn't matter what happens." Forcing a smile, she shoved open the car door.

As she stepped onto the sidewalk, the office windows reflected the street behind her, obscuring her view of the inside. In the warped glass, she saw a man toss a cigarette then step into a car. Her skin prickled with goose bumps, but he was pulling away, hidden behind dark-tinted windows, before she could place him.

Reminding herself to smile—again—Ivy turned to the office door. Bells jingled as she opened it. The office was just as she'd expected: gray carpeting, lots of houseplants, and a slick reception desk. The blinds were open, letting in the natural light.

A youngish woman with chocolate-brown hair pulled up into a perky ponytail looked up from the open laptop on her desk. "Hiya! You must be Ivy." Her infectious smiled quelled Ivy's nervousness. The woman stood and shook Ivy's hand, even though Ivy didn't realize she'd even extended her own hand.

Ivy nodded. "Uh, yes."

"Nice to meet you. I'm Karen. Mark should be back here in a few."

"Great." Ivy's brain went into autopilot, conjuring small talk about the weather and college in response to Karen's friendly chatter. Then she sat quietly while Karen took phone calls, always in her rushed, cheerful tone.

Finally, a man much younger than Ivy had expected breezed through the door, shoving sunglasses up into his reddish hair. Her pulse sped up when she noticed how close the color of his hair was to her own, but she pushed that thought aside. *He can't be, remember?*

As soon as he spotted her, his eyes lit up. "Hello, Ivy." He extended his hand, fixing his hypnotic green gaze on her. "Nice to meet you. Karen said you were coming in about the job."

After an awkward handshake, he led her to a desk in the corner and pulled out a chair for her. As he sat on the other side, he flashed her an intoxicating smile, complete with dimples, making her heart flutter. *Wow, I'll bet this guy sells a lot of houses. The picture certainly didn't do him justice.*

"So you're interested in selling houses, Ivy? Or are you just hoping to get some experience under your belt while you're looking into other things?" He gave her a sly wink that she wasn't sure how to interpret.

She spent the next half hour stumbling through answers to questions and managing a few of her own. All the while, she forced down the urge to ask him questions about her mother. He didn't ask a single question about her family. *Is that because he already knows who I am or because he thinks I don't know who he is?*

Mark leaned forward, resting his chin in his hand as if to study her. Finally, he nodded. "I think you'll be great for the job. Sometimes I'll need you to come along with me to open houses and sales. Other times, we'll need you here at the office to help Karen. What do you think?"

Despite the knots in her stomach, a girlish smile forced its way across her face. "Sounds great."

"Well, we're actually about to go out of town for a bit. How does starting in two weeks sound?"

"Good," she answered, still struggling to maintain her composure in proximity to his intense presence. *You cannot have a crush on this man, Ivy.* That was weird for several reasons.

After Karen signed off on the new hire, they said their goodbyes. Ivy drove home with a renewed sense of purpose, feeling as if she might have gotten a little closer to a clue about her mother. Mostly, though, she tried not to think about Mark Morrison's stare.

As Ivy pulled into the driveway at the farmhouse, she spotted her grandmother ushering a group of children onto a school bus parked near the barn. After a brief wave to the bus driver, Audrey started over to Ivy's car.

"Summer camp tour?" Ivy asked.

"Of course." Audrey grinned. "The kids seem to look younger and younger every year. Must be getting old." She gave Ivy a wink as they stepped onto the porch. "So how did the meeting go?"

Despite her earlier lack of enthusiasm, a bubble of excitement rose in her throat. "He offered me the job. I start in a couple of weeks."

"That's wonderful." Audrey squeezed Ivy's shoulder. "We can celebrate later. But right now, why don't you come help me in the garden?"

"Just let me get changed," Ivy called as she jogged toward the house. Inside, it smelled of baking and strong tea, as it always did. *That smell could sell plenty of houses,* she thought, smiling. Then she caught herself wondering what Mark's house smelled like. *Stop it!*

In her room, Ivy slipped off her shoes and kicked them into the open closet. A shuffling sound in the doorway told her she wasn't alone. She turned to find Violet leaning against the jamb.

"Mark Morrison, huh?" Violet asked, a sharp tone to her voice. Her lips twitched as if she were holding back a sneer.

Heavy silence filled the room while Ivy simply stared at her sister, meeting her gaze. She squelched the panic that had begun to tingle in her sternum. Regardless of Ivy's best efforts to avoid an argument with Violet, her sister had sniffed her out anyhow.

Finally, Violet broke the tense hush. "I know what this is about."

"It's about I needed a job. I can't sit around here all day, doing nothing."

Violet's eyes narrowed. "It's about Rachel."

How did she know?

"Everybody knows. He's probably just as sick of the gossip as we are."

"*I* didn't know."

"You haven't been here." Her voice carried the hint of restrained frustration. "Of course you wouldn't know."

"I'm sorry," was all Ivy could muster. Anything else would only add fuel to the fire.

The flicker of sadness in Violet's eyes gave way to anger. "She's not coming back. You've been back for, like, five minutes, and the only person here you want anything to do with is Mark Morrison. Are you trying to *be* her now?" Violet winced as though reacting to the acidity of her own words, but Ivy didn't answer. "She didn't... I just... why can't you let it go? Just let *her* go?"

"I just wanted a job," Ivy croaked past the lump in her throat.

Violet shook her head and turned to leave. "Whatever. Just don't do this to Gran." She walked away, leaving a shimmering pocket of anger in her wake.

Ivy sank onto the bed, holding back tears. Then she took a deep breath and shoved all of her remorse deep into the pit of her stomach where she kept the rest of her regrets.

Chapter Eight

VIOLET STOOD AT THE MARKET counter with her checkbook open, scribbling out the check. Wendy, the older woman who seemed to work every shift at the grocery store, was particularly chatty that day.

"A nice-looking man asked after you the other day, Violet." A self-satisfied glimmer in her eye, she made a show of looking around to make sure no one would hear, even though she made no attempt to lower the volume of her voice.

"Oh, yeah?" Violet joked absentmindedly without looking up from what she was writing. "Did he look rich? Maybe he's my new boyfriend." She winked as she handed over the check. She'd grown accustomed to both the gossip and being its subject, and she assumed Wendy was referring to Kevin.

"He must have some money." Wendy leaned in as if she were bestowing a big secret upon Violet. Her large clip-on earrings dangled dramatically. "He bought the house on the edge of town. The one that belonged to Libby Walsh. That's a real nice house, one of the historic homes, you know."

"You don't know his name?" Violet asked, her interest piqued. Wendy was *not* talking about Kevin.

"Oh, I wasn't here, dear. Dan was." Wendy stuffed bags into the cart. "If he said a name, Dan didn't tell me. Dan said this guy just asked if you were ever in town and how you and your family were doing, like he knew you and such. I was hoping you might tell me who he was. I know it wasn't your policeman friend." She elbowed Violet playfully.

Violet smiled sheepishly on cue. "So I suppose you don't know what he looked like either, then?" Violet wracked her brain for who he could possibly be. *Rich guy? I don't know any rich guys.*

"No, dear," Wendy said. "I tell you what, though. I'll find out for you."

"Where did Mrs. Walsh move?" Violet asked.

Libby Walsh was one of the town's most prominent members of society. She wasn't exactly frail enough to need a nursing home—her yard, which she tended herself, won the hometown pride award from the Town Gardener's Association almost every year—and she had never seemed the kind of lady who would downgrade to smaller accommodations, whether or not she needed the space. She hosted the Tour of Homes at Christmastime and always invited everyone in for cider on Halloween.

An unexpected flash of realization crossed Wendy's face. "You know, I don't know..." Despite her usual proclivity for chatting regardless of whether a line formed at her checkout station, distress filled her widened eyes when she glanced at the customers waiting behind Violet. She smiled nervously. "I'll have to find that out for you, too."

"Thanks, Wendy." Violet took off out the door with her purchases, wondering whether or not that might have been the strange man who had been lurking on the farm a few days before. *That guy was a little too pudgy to be "nice looking..."*

Her thoughts dissolved as she caught sight of the young man who was headed toward her with a smile on his face. Violet thought about how much nicer Kevin Bonniere looked in a T-shirt and jeans than he did his police uniform. His short, blond hair was sun bleached and looked nearly white in contrast to his tanned skin and dark eyes. His pace hastened when he saw that she had seen him.

"Hey, Violet," he said, catching up to her at the door of her truck. "How's things going out at your place? No new visitors I need to check out?" Dimples crinkled at the edges of his smile.

They had been at that same game for a while, going out of the way to run into each other and talk. Neither had worked up the courage to do anything about what was clearly obvious to the small town's many observers, who didn't hide the fact that they were watching the pretty girl and attractive young new officer. Violet's frustration with the situation simmered at the surface, making her itch.

"No, just the usual." She opened the passenger door of the old truck, which protested with a squeak. "But you're welcome to come check things out anytime you like." She smiled at him coyly, and a light blush crept up his neck.

He recovered right away, though, clearing his throat. "Well, maybe I'll take you up on that offer sometime." Laughing, he reached across the cart to help her load the bags of groceries into the truck. "I've been thinking maybe we should get together sometime when I'm not on duty." He shuffled his feet, studying the bubbled tar on the parking lot asphalt as if it were suddenly very interesting.

Finally!

"But seriously," he continued, assuming his police posture and tone of voice as he looked up to meet her eyes, "we never really did figure out who that guy was. We asked around, and no one recognized his description. Doesn't sound like he's a local."

"It's not unusual that we'll get people stopping by to buy things we don't have ready yet or just appearing because they got lost out on the country roads." Violet shrugged, disappointed that he seemed so intent on discussing business instead of more personal things. "This guy was just extra strange." *And then there's the magic.* She thought maybe one day she could tell Kevin about that, but the middle of the grocery store parking lot was not the place. One of the tellers from the bank hurried past, no doubt running errands on her break, and waved, a knowing smile on her face. Violet waved back, forcing her fake smile all the way to her eyes.

"Yeah, it concerns me a little bit. It's a good thing that you ladies have Sam out there, but maybe remind him to be more careful running out to confront guys like that." Kevin's protective tone reminded Violet of Grandpa Jack.

They had finished loading the bags, and he pushed the door shut for her. He also grabbed the handle of the cart. "I'll take this up on my way in." He gestured toward the store. "And I'll give you a call soon about, well, *not* public safety." He broke into a wide smile that creased his face and made his dark eyes sparkle.

"Okay," Violet chirped, resisting the urge to giggle girlishly. She offered him what she hoped was a pleasant smile instead. She was a little too breathless to be certain she looked pleasant. *Probably just sweaty.*

"Good." He nodded. "Good." Pushing the cart, he continued his journey to the store. Violet stood watching him walk away, and he glanced back and gave her a small half wave. She raised her hand back at him and smiled again, suddenly aware of the other shoppers in the parking lot, who had followed his line of sight back to where she was standing, looking silly. She and Kevin would no doubt be the topic of discussion in the store for the rest of the day. Wendy would certainly be pleased.

Violet scrambled into the truck and took off. When there wasn't much excitement in town, gossip was always cheap entertainment. *It's harmless,* she thought. However, she made a mental note to check out the house on the edge of town sometime.

"Oh, what the hell?" she whispered when she pulled up to the edge of the street. She jerked the wheel toward Libby Walsh's house. "Might as well get in on the gossip."

As she drove, her mind wandered, mostly toward thoughts of Kevin Bonniere and his white T-shirts, and she found herself losing interest in the curious new occupant at the Walsh mansion. Stopped at the intersection at the end of the street leading to the house, Violet glanced toward the home. With a shrug, she dismissed the house entirely and turned, pointing the hood of her truck in the direction of her own house.

Ivy climbed out of bed and stretched, feeling as if she might have actually slept for an entire night. Just maybe the dreams had run their course. After getting dressed, she stood at the window, looking out at the lawn sparkling with dew. The residual magic left behind by the farm's unusual visitor had finally dissipated.

The sound of her grandmother singing drew her attention away from the window. She followed it downstairs, where Audrey was singing as she bustled around the kitchen, stacking things in the cabinets.

Ivy poked her head around the corner. "Hey, Gran, what do you have planned today?"

"I have a bunch of stuff to do around the house. It would be wonderful if you wanted to take my place and go with Violet to the strawberry festival. She'll probably need the help, and you can catch up with some of the people you haven't seen since you got home."

Unimpressed with the prospect of socializing, Ivy rolled her eyes but took up a rag and joined her grandmother in wiping down the counters. "I hate trying to talk to people I haven't seen in a long time. It's weird."

Audrey turned toward her with a sour look on her face. "You'll need the practice if you think you're going to sell houses."

Ivy raised her arms and let them flop at her sides in a half-hearted shrug. "What exactly would she need me to do?"

"Setting up and helping with money and such. I already put names on the special orders, but the rest are pretzels and strawberry tarts and things. She's in the office. Why don't you go ask?"

Ivy headed for the office, running her hand along the wallpaper textured with raised pink roses. Near the doorway to the office, she came up against a palpable buzz that seemed to always accompany Violet's states of concentration. It slipped across Ivy's skin, tickling the hairs on her arms.

Leaning through the doorway, she rapped a knuckle on the open door. "Hey, Vi."

"What's up?" Violet asked without looking up. "I'm about finished here."

Ivy looked around the room and hovered next to a chair piled with binders. She considered moving them then thought better of the idea. Biting back a snide comment about the state of the office, she peered over Violet's shoulder.

Violet looked up with a frown as if she knew Ivy was about to offer up unsolicited advice. "Yes?"

"Gran said you might want some help later on."

Violet spun enthusiastically in the office chair. "That would be great. If it's slow, I end up standing around by myself. If it's busy, then I'm going crazy." She whirled around, setting her pen atop an open garden-supply catalog. Static crackled across the air as Violet thought for a moment. "Come on. I need to get stuff packed anyway. It's getting late." She jumped up and grabbed Ivy's hands, zapping her with a jolt of electricity. She pulled Ivy to her feet and dragged her out of the room.

Violet had already packed an old folding table into the back of the truck, and Ivy helped her stack wooden crates filled with fruit and baked goods atop it before they set off. Ivy watched the verdant landscape passing outside the window of the truck. Here and there, aging brown grass dotted the side of the roads where the new growth hadn't quite overpowered the old yet.

Ivy peered into the rearview mirror to check that nothing seemed amiss. A few handwritten tags whipped in the wind, but their load was otherwise stable. She turned to fiddle with the radio out of boredom. Her efforts were rewarded with a static hiss on nearly every channel as she spun the dial.

"It doesn't work anymore. The antenna's broken," Violet said. "Gran and I tried to fix it. That didn't work out." She smiled. "It was bent, and she tried to straighten it. The thing broke completely off."

"Yeah, you guys break a lot of stuff," Ivy teased. She looked out at the antenna, which was, indeed, just a stump. She punched the eject button on the cassette player just to see what the tape was. Nothing happened.

"She also got an Otis Redding tape stuck in there," Violet said, sounding amused.

"Otis Redding?" Ivy scrunched up her face. "Since when does Gran like Otis Redding?"

"Well, she probably likes him a little less since that's been stuck in there," Violet answered wryly. "It still plays if you want to listen to it."

"Not really." Ivy settled back into her seat and watched the rounded hills of countryside slowly passing by. Clumps of trees and grazing cows, each one wearing a dangling identification tag in its ear, broke up the monotony of the green fields. Marshall County really was pretty in the summer, but she was too anxious to admit it. Unwilling to continue the ride in silence, Ivy brought up a new subject. "So you and the hot cop guy, huh?"

"I dunno," Violet answered without hesitation, as if she'd been thinking of him anyway. "I think so, but not yet. We're kind of stuck in this awkward stage where we're just really friendly to each other." She grimaced at the steering wheel and shrugged. "Maybe he's just being nice."

"I don't think so. Everyone else seems to have noticed how 'friendly' you are." Ivy had overheard two women she didn't know discussing her sister while waiting in line to order coffee. That moment had stung for two reasons. First, the women obviously hadn't recognized her as Violet's sister. And second, Violet hadn't told her about this major thing going on in her life. The possibility of a relationship seemed important to Ivy, anyway. *Maybe not so much to Violet. She probably has lots of guys after her.* "Why didn't you ever mention him to me before?"

"Because it's weird and embarrassing. You know how it is—everybody has to get their little digs in, and it starts to feel like everyone else knows more about it than I do." She laughed lightly as she said it, but Ivy heard the passive bitterness that crept into her cheerful tone. "We used to talk about stuff like that all the time, but after you left, you never told me about any guys, so I guess I thought we maybe didn't talk about that kind of thing anymore." Violet pulled her eyes from the road for a brief second to gauge her sister's reaction.

"I just never had anything to report, I guess." She shifted nervously, recalling her own attempts—all failures—at romance. "I suck at dating, and I'm terrible at parties. I really only attracted weirdos… so I gave up. I thought if it was going to happen, it would have." She shrugged, trying to play down the feeling of failure creeping into the spaces between her lungs. "I'd kind of thought that boys at college would be different. Maybe somewhere, they are."

"I doubt it. Besides, I think it's pretty here, and we have a business and a nice house."

Ivy picked up on the violent swing in the direction of the conversation.

"And Gran is here… she's really all we have, you know?" Raising an eyebrow, Violet looked away from her sister and out at the corn that grew just beyond the fencerows at the edge of the road. "We are all she has, too. If you leave, and I leave…" She trailed off into a shrug.

Even with Violet's sentence unfinished, Ivy knew what she meant. Audrey would be alone if they both left. Violet pointed that out every time Ivy brought up their mother.

Ivy shook her head to clear away her thoughts. "Oh, well. That's enough pity party for today. Why don't you tell me some more about Hot Cop Guy."

"Well, his name's Kevin, first off. He started working for the sheriff's office about eight or nine months ago. He's from Louisiana—"

"How did he end up all the way up here?" She cocked her head to the side. No one ever seemed to move *to* Marshall County, only away. "That does explain the accent, though."

"He inherited a house—the two-story brick one, kind of around the corner from the library and the funeral home."

"Oh, yeah?" Ivy whistled through her teeth. "That's a nice house. I don't even know who used to live there. Never looked empty, though."

"Mr. Glasson, who used to run the café, lived there, but apparently, he only rented it. He went to a nursing home about a year before Kevin inherited the house. The owner died. That's obvious, I guess. It's not like he's evasive about it, but he always manages to never really answer when I ask who owned it. So I took that to mean he doesn't want to talk about it."

"Cryptic…" Ivy murmured.

Violet rolled her eyes.

"Well, it is." Ivy shrugged. "He seems nice, though."

"Yeah. He is nice," she said tersely, as if announcing she was finished with the subject if Ivy wasn't going to be helpful. "Are you excited about the *festivities*? You get to see everyone in town, tell everyone what it's like in the city."

"Yeah, right, like anybody cares about that stuff." Ivy hadn't quite admitted to even her twin that she hadn't seen much of the city beyond the college campus, which was really more like the suburbs, and she wasn't sure she'd seen all of that, either. Her job in the college library had only aided her ability to lurk in quiet places without talking to people or seeing new things. Missed opportunities seemed to haunt her wherever she went. Taking the job with Mark Morrison was a step in the right direction.

"They might." Violet let the tense conversation wander off into silence. The sound of the wind rushing past the cab, whistling in around the old weather stripping of the windows, took over the rest of the ride.

The square looked so different when it was dressed up for a festival. Ivy hadn't been to the homecoming or anything like that in a few years, and an unexpected longing for her hometown crept up from the soles of her shoes as she stepped out of the truck and onto the gravel parking lot of the Presbyterian church at the corner of the square.

Violet smiled at her over the hood of the truck, and Ivy smiled back. She might not feel at home anywhere, but she knew where she felt loved. Buoyed by a conscious effort to be positive that day, she started around the truck to unload their wares.

Chapter Nine

CHARLIE LOGAN WAS CARRYING ON a friendly conversation with a pretty young woman—she had introduced herself, but he didn't care—all the while keeping an eye on Ivy Grant, who was watching her sister talk with a young man. Anywhere Charlie went these days, he hoped to find Ivy there. He'd come back to Oak Hill just for her, after all. It was the first time he'd seen her since returning to town, though. He'd started to think she'd run off, just like her mother had. But hope would always spring eternal—and his perseverance had finally been rewarded.

Ivy was all grown-up. She looked just like she did in his dreams. He'd dreamt of her more and more often over the last few months, sometimes so vividly that he felt as if he were there with her, watching her sleep. Her hair was still the lovely, deep reddish-brown that reminded him of thick maple syrup. An image of her as a child flashed across his mind: the sun shining on her perfect mahogany braid. He'd wanted desperately to unwind it and twine it between his fingers.

She had cut her hair short so that it barely hung past her chin, but her perfect skin was just how he remembered. He imagined her in the barn, where against the dark T-shirt and faded jeans cut into shorts, her skin had seemed to glow in the light filtering through the slats of the barn's wall while she'd played with the kittens. Charlie liked how girls always seemed drawn to kittens. Violet had never shared Ivy's interest in kittens, and that made him like the other girl even less. A grimace crossed his face at the thought of Ivy's dark-haired twin, then he forced a smile as he jerked himself back to reality.

He was desperate to blend in with the town and hoped that he might be able to win Ivy over with his newfound "charms." But she knew him in a way none of the others did. He wondered how much she actually remembered him—if at all. He might have been nothing more than a fleeting memory in her life, but thoughts of her still consumed him.

His gaze flitted back to the woman speaking to him. She couldn't have missed the fact that he hadn't responded, let alone looked directly at her, in minutes. *How has she not noticed?* Or perhaps he'd been staring for only a second and it just *seemed* like forever. He checked his watch. A full five minutes had passed since the woman had asked him what time the band was supposed to start their set. He decided his spell was working perfectly and congratulated himself on the small victory. Whenever people looked at him—or his house—they seemed to see what they wanted to see.

The evening sun had begun to sink behind the courthouse on the square, and the streetlights were glowing. While Ivy was distracted watching Violet, the circle of conversation that Ivy was a part of drifted away from her. Charlie saw his opportunity.

He glanced over at Violet, whose attention was focused entirely on a tall, blond young man. Sizing up the younger man, Charlie thought he might hold his own in a fight with him. But the man was not after Charlie Logan's prize. Charlie had no interest in fighting for Violet Grant. His lip started to pull into a sneer before he squelched it. *How could any man think Violet's attractive?* As a child, Violet had reminded him of a jackrabbit, always stopping to ponder things before tearing off toward her next interest. Her busyness made him anxious. She gave him the impression that she was underfoot—or about to be—even when she was nowhere near. The girl had tended to suddenly appear with questions, a weather report, or God knew what. Grown-up, she was all sharp edges and opinions.

Satisfied that Violet was appropriately occupied, he turned away. The blond woman, a determined conversationalist, had moved into his new line of sight and was only inches from his face when he turned back. Resisting the urge to shove her out of the way, he attempted to feign interest in what she was saying as he laid his hand on her arm and gently moved her away.

"Officer Bonniere seems to have taken a liking to Violet Grant," she said in a desperate bid to keep his attention. "I always thought that whole family was just a little odd, you know?" She stumbled on the redbrick sidewalk and teetered a little, blocking his view of Ivy. He squeezed her arm just a little too hard as he brusquely pulled her upright. She winced, and the small action nearly set him off.

Clenching his fists at his sides, he swallowed the urge to shove her down to the ground and order her out of his way. He reminded himself that he was supposed to be charming. Any other day, he might have enjoyed the pretty lady's company. He stretched his neck and took a deep breath. Ivy hadn't gone far—she was still drifting in and out of the conversation, but she hadn't noticed him.

Forcing a smile, he said, "I'm sorry. Watch out for the, uh, loose brick there. Look, I see someone I need to say hello to. It was nice talking to you."

"Oh, of course. Give me a ca—"

He simply walked away since the young woman hadn't understood that she'd been dismissed. Making a conscious effort to not seem as if he were skulking or making a beeline toward Ivy, he weaved through the crowd. His eyes left her only to see if Violet had noticed him. He didn't know if Violet would even recognize him, but that girl had always been like a wild animal. And wild animals were unpredictable.

After a day spent selling pies, jams, and other baked things that Ivy was certain would pack on the pounds, she had wandered away from the Grant Farms stand, hoping to find some peace. Nearly everything they'd brought was sold out, and despite all the forced small talk she'd managed during the day, Ivy still found herself caught up in more chitchat after an old classmate spotted her. Hanna Gordon apparently thought Ivy had been a better friend to her than Ivy remembered being. Ivy didn't really remember having any of her own friends—they had all belonged to Violet.

Ivy's eyes strayed back to the stand, where Kevin Bonniere was helping Violet pack up. For a second, she had a wispy, wistful feeling, wishing that she had an attractive young man to rescue her from the constant dread of managing conversation with people whose faces she vaguely recognized but couldn't actually remember. They all treated her as if she should know everything that had been going on in her absence, not really leaving her out of the conversation but simply carrying on without her. They weren't rude—everyone she'd talked to that day had been unexpectedly friendly— but keeping up with the flow was exhausting. Her brain was starting to get foggy. Still, she was determined to hang in there until the band started. *And I should probably give Violet a chance to talk with Kevin.* Realizing she'd scrunched her face into what had to be an unfriendly expression, she relaxed and started to turn back to her companions.

"Hey there, Ivy," a man whispered. He was standing uncomfortably close to her.

She hadn't heard that voice in nearly half a lifetime. She hadn't expected to ever hear it again. Some days, she didn't even remember ever having heard it. But the dread from that single day, that single chain of moments, immediately filled her heart. She could still see his face, too close to hers, distorted by the shafts of light filtering in through the boards of the barn's walls. Magic, the same as she'd felt in the yard the week before, smothered her. All at once, she knew the source of the dread that had followed her home. *No, it can't be!*

She froze, unable to react. Even though she was surrounded by people, the world spun away from her. In the few seconds that she had turned away to look for Violet, the circle of conversation had slipped past her, leaving her slightly adjacent to the group, outside its protective borders. The streetlights seemed far away. The voices around her died to murmurs. The breathy voice behind her was all that existed. An intense, buzzing tingle vibrated the air around her. She wished the suffocating sensation could shield her. She called out silently for her sister.

Hesitant to face him dead-on, she half turned so that she could see him only in the corner of her vision. The smell of stale cigarette smoke and old coffee mixed with the heavy evening air as it wafted by her. Charlie Logan stood behind her with a wide, friendly grin on his face. His white teeth seemed to glow in the evening light against the tan of his skin. He hadn't changed much over the years. The wan streetlights cast menacing shadows over his features, making him seem disfigured. His hair was shot with salt and pepper.

He pushed one hand into the pocket of his blue jeans. His other hand hugged his opposite arm to his side. The rolled sleeve of his dark button-down shirt pulled up to reveal the bottom edges of a tattoo that she could not fully discern. She stood staring at him like a feral cat wishing her calico markings could blend into the green grass—if she could only stand still enough and never take her eyes away.

"You're so grown-up now," he said sweetly. "Still so pretty." He reached out his hand to touch her hair.

She jerked back as if his hand were a snake. Her arm instinctively flew up past her face to knock it away.

A look of hurt and confusion flickered across his face. Ivy couldn't imagine what sort of response he had expected from her. The dark look that followed lasted only a second. Ivy thought she had imagined it—almost. Charlie's eyes glided across the crowd, no doubt looking for anyone who might have witnessed Ivy's reaction. He was like an abusive husband who suddenly realized that others might take notice of his victim's behavior.

The second that his eyes left her, Ivy swiftly stepped away.

"Ivy, what's wrong?" Hanna's voice injected relief into Ivy's heart.

As her tunnel vision widened to include Hanna, Ivy returned to the reality of the crowded town square. Her lemon shake-up had spilled onto the pavement in front of her. But her lungs were capable of taking in oxygen again.

Hanna touched Ivy's arm gingerly. With concerned eyes, she searched Ivy's face. "Are you okay? You look like you saw a ghost."

Ivy turned back to Charlie, but he had backed away and melted into the crowd.

"Oh, I just..." She grasped for words, knowing she couldn't possibly explain everything. "Do you know that guy?" she asked, catching sight of Charlie among the other people in the crowded square and pointing. "With the dark shirt and jeans right there."

"Oh, yeah." Hanna tucked a lock of her blond hair behind her ear coquettishly. "Well, I've seen him around lately, and I'd like to know him better, if you know what I mean." She fanned her face with her hand, feigning overheating. "I heard he bought that big house on Turner Road, where the Walsh lady lived. Charlie Logan, I think, is his name."

"Oh, I, um... oh, okay." She forced herself to swallow even though her mouth was dry. Pretty young Hanna Gordon shouldn't have considered Charlie Logan an eligible bachelor. Something was wrong. She felt a spell or some other magic tugging at her, but she tucked that thought away for later. "He surprised me, I guess."

Casting furtive glances back at Ivy, Charlie was chatting cheerfully with a gray-haired woman who was obviously taken with him. Charlie was not disfigured at all and was, in fact, attractive. Only her knowledge of his advances toward a shy little girl all those years ago made him dreadful. An ugly thought struck her. *Where has he been all these years? And who else has he touched?* Fear and panic blossomed around her, threatening to overtake her while she struggled to maintain a composed demeanor.

"I'd better go help Violet. She must need me by now."

Hanna nodded, but the look on the young woman's face told Ivy that her panic was obvious. "I'll see you soon, okay. You have my number?"

"Yeah. See ya." Ivy smiled at Hanna, but her eyes were already searching the crowd for Violet.

Under the wooden pavilion at the center of the town square, members of a bluegrass band were tuning their instruments. As the sun started its slow, sinking glide behind the western horizon, Violet surveyed her wares, which were nearly gone. Never had she ever sold all of the rhubarb jelly, but Audrey always insisted that she try.

"Damn rhubarb!" she said. Violet locked the cash into a metal box, which she placed into the bottom of a milk crate, and stacked the remaining jars of jam and a couple of wrapped pretzels on top of it. She exchanged waves and hellos with several people who passed as she settled the crate onto the small dolly.

"Hey, Violet!" A scrawny teenage boy jogged up to her side.

Oh, Austin, it ain't gonna happen. Violet was more embarrassed by the boy's crush than he was. Still, he was mostly a good kid, so she did her best to be polite and hoped she wasn't encouraging him. "What's up?"

"Nothing much. Lookin' forward to the music. You?" Hands in his pockets, he rocked onto his tiptoes out of nervous habit.

She turned to grab the tablecloth off the folding table. Austin's hands flew out of his pockets so fast that Violet was amazed he hadn't ripped the front out of his jeans.

"Oh, here. I'll get that." He snatched up the other end of the cloth then proceeded to do a haphazard job of folding it, which amounted to little more than wadding it up tightly.

"Thanks," she said, accepting the bundled tablecloth.

Austin's eyes were eager for praise. *Poor kid. I wonder if anybody at home appreciates him at all—or even notices him.* His good intentions cascaded off him in palpable waves—the everyday kind of magic that Violet wished everyone could feel. She tucked the cloth into an empty space in the crate and picked up the leftover pretzels. "How about you take these, maybe share one with a pretty girl?" In a serious tone, she added, "Not me."

His bravado deflated. "Thanks, Violet. Are you sure you don't need any more help?" He took the pretzels.

"No, thanks. I appreciate the offer, though. Really." She smiled. "If you stick around much longer, I'll make you take the rhubarb jelly."

"Gross." He took off, giving her a wave over his shoulder. "I'll see you later, maybe."

"Yeah, okay." She smiled then looked fleetingly for her sister. Violet hoped that Ivy was rediscovering her niche in their hometown. The restless tension that Ivy exuded constantly mingled with Violet's selfish concern that Ivy would disrupt her happy existence, but she hated the thought of her sister leaving again.

She carefully flipped the long table onto its edge so that she could fold the legs up under it, and it wobbled awkwardly. She realized that she was going to need help carrying it back to the truck. *Crap. Should've kept Austin around.*

Again, she looked up, wondering if Ivy was nearby. Instead of her sister, she spotted Kevin walking toward her. An unstoppable grin spread across her face. As he came closer, his eyes flickered self-consciously away from hers, and he became intensely focused on planting his feet in precise locations in the grass.

"Hey," he said. "Do you need help with any of that?" Without waiting for an answer, he grasped the table edge and leaned it toward himself, ready to heft it.

"Yeah, I do." Violet's giddy smile lingered. "I was just wondering how I was going to carry all of this." She swept her arm over the table and crates on the dolly.

"Well, here—you get that," he said softly as he pointed to the end of the table, "and I'll grab this and this." He pulled the dolly over to him and gripped the far end of the table beneath his arm. "Lead the way."

Violet lifted her end of the table, then they made their way down the alley between the old brick buildings to the parking lot where her truck was waiting. The sun had finally faded from the sky, and the nearly full moon hung close to the earth, pulling at her. After they had loaded the table into the back of the truck, Violet unlocked the door of the cab. She pointed to the crate with the cash box. "I need that crate in here," she said, opening the door.

Kevin grabbed it and moved in to push it across the bench seat, his body close to hers. The smell of his soap, and the urge to kiss him, overwhelmed her. She hesitated then reached out to touch his arm. Static shock shot across her skin. He met her eyes, his eyebrows raised in surprise. In the half of a heartbeat that he hesitated, Violet feared that she had made a mistake.

Then he pressed against her as he leaned in to kiss her. The cold, hard steel of the truck warmed against her back. His muscles were tense, but he relaxed as she kissed him back. She felt conspicuous at first, but then the outside world melted away under the heat of his body. Winding her arms around his waist, she pulled him to her tighter, her hands spread across the straining muscles of his back. His fingers tangled in her hair.

An anxious pressure built inside Violet's chest. As it pushed its way through the fog of hormones that clouded her head, she began to recognize its source. Somewhere close, her sister was looking for her. And she was afraid. Ivy's fear became impossible to ignore, and Violet's own fear mixed with it. She pushed Kevin away abruptly.

His face flushed scarlet red. "I'm sorry." He moved away, his eyes locked on the gravel where they stood.

"No," Violet said, grabbing his arm to prevent him from pulling away. "I didn't mean to… I need to find Ivy." She stammered over an explanation of the panic that had momentarily overwhelmed her. "I forgot about her. I was supposed to meet her. I don't know what time it is…"

The confusion in his eyes melted. He inhaled as if he'd only just then remembered how to breathe.

"Just come with me, okay? Don't leave." Still holding his forearm, she started to walk away.

"Sure." He awkwardly slapped at the lock on the truck door and slammed it shut as she dragged him away.

Violet scanned the crowd as she walked, following the silver thread of fear strung tautly between her and Ivy. She imagined how stupid she must look, wandering through a crowd without speaking to any of them and towing a man behind her. Consumed by the need to find her sister, she stifled that concern, but she let go of Kevin.

Then she lost the connection. She wasn't sure what she was following or if she *had* been simply wandering in a blind panic. The square—hell, the town—wasn't that big. "Where is she?" She faltered. Then Kevin pointed.

Ivy was walking toward them at a brisk pace, her eyes wide and focused entirely on Violet.

Matching her sister's pace, Violet started in her direction. As soon as she was within reach, Ivy grabbed Violet and pulled her close. Violet wrapped her sister in a hug and squeezed. Ivy's chest heaved with a sob though she didn't make a sound.

"What happened?" Violet asked. "I thought you were just talking. I'm sorry."

They were suddenly children again, huddled in a hug in the foyer with their grandmother while Ivy struggled to explain. And Violet understood the emotions that she had seen on her grandmother's face as she'd stormed out of the house and headed toward the barn. Guilt, anger, and fear mixed into a caustic fuel that threatened to burn up her veins if she didn't expend it immediately with action. But she stood still and let it burn because Ivy didn't release her grip.

Finally, Ivy pulled away to look Violet in the eye. Surprisingly, Ivy wasn't in tears. Violet could sense the panic again, but Ivy had reeled it in securely to her core. *Damn, she's good at that.* Ivy's ability to hide so her emotions was impressive—and Violet wondered how much her sister was always hiding.

"Charlie Logan is here," she whispered. "And I think he's using magic. It's the magic from the yard."

"What? That doesn't make sense. Are you sure?" She'd practically forgotten about the guy in yard, which was odd, especially since his magic had lingered. *When did that happen?* Violet felt Kevin's hand on her arm and looked over at him. He cocked his head to the side discreetly, gesturing for them to follow him back to the truck.

With a hand on her sister's back, Violet put Ivy between herself and Kevin. Taking another look around the crowd, she didn't see anyone suspicious. She struggled to recall an image of Charlie Logan. Everything she remembered about him was clouded by a vision of her grandmother that day. Her grandmother's expression. Audrey standing in the yard, fuming with hatred. The blind rage and panic that Violet had been too young to put words to at the time.

She forced herself back to the present. Kevin was leading them toward the truck. The crowd was already behind them.

In front of the truck, he turned to them. "Is everything okay? That looked like a big deal."

The air around them buzzed as Violet's own emotions rose to the surface. She concentrated on relaxing. Charlie Logan was merely a man. She and Ivy were grown women who knew how to handle themselves—and Charlie had aged. He wouldn't be able to do much with Kevin standing there, anyway. Only her imagination had made him into a monster. He was horrible, but he was just a man. *But what about the magic? Is he connected to the other man?* Violet wished she had a comforting answer to go along with those questions.

Kevin waited patiently but with expectation painted all over his demeanor. His back rigid, he'd shifted into police mode.

"There's just this guy who caused us some trouble back when Ivy was a little girl. It was, uh… inappropriate." Violet wasn't sure how much Ivy wanted anyone to know, even though not much had really happened. Still, Violet's own reaction to his presence told her Charlie Logan had affected them more than she wanted to admit. "He showed up and talked to Ivy just now."

Kevin rubbed the back of his neck nervously and nodded. "Do you need me to follow you home in my car?" He jerked his thumb in the direction of a Ford Escort that had seen better days. "I assume you're going home, not hanging around here." Violet caught a hint of disappointment in his voice, but she had to agree that going home would be the best plan.

Ivy shook her head. "He didn't actually say anything threatening. It was just so strange that he thought he could walk up and talk to me like that. I think we'll be all right to get home."

Kevin bid them farewell, giving Violet a kiss on the cheek and Ivy a simple goodbye. He waited for them to get in the truck and leave the parking lot before getting into his own vehicle. She watched him for a second, thinking about his body pressed against hers. *Charlie Logan, you son of a bitch.*

Violet reached across the seat for her sister's hand. "Gran will know what to do, I'm sure."

They held hands in silence as they rode home in the darkness. It was nearly ten o'clock when Violet pulled up into the drive. Audrey had left the porch light on for them, but the house was mostly dark. The truck's headlights caught the mirrors hung on the house, bouncing beams across the yard at sharp angles. The scene was just eerie enough to make Violet wish she had asked Kevin to follow them home. *Come on. You've been to your own house after dark before.*

"Looks like Gran's already gone to bed," Ivy said.

Violet nodded, shutting off the engine. "Yeah, she's not really a night owl, even in the summer." She grabbed the door handle, making sure she had her house key at the ready. No matter how lax they were about locking the door during the day, whether they were home or not, it was always locked at night. "Ready?" she asked Ivy as if they were about to make a break for the door.

Ivy nodded and jumped out of the passenger side of the truck. She hustled around the front of the vehicle as Violet got out on her side. Neither of them ran toward the door, but they were just short of speed walking.

As soon as Violet unlocked the door, they rushed inside. Their grandmother had, indeed, gone to bed and left the light on in the kitchen. Violet locked the door behind her and turned to Ivy. "You going to sleep?"

Ivy crossed her arms over her chest, hugging herself. "I don't know. I might go read or something."

"You want to wake Gran?" Violet asked. Charlie Logan might not have been much more than a pervert who could be handled with a swift kick to the nether regions, but she couldn't deny that something strange had happened at the farm. And if Ivy said she'd felt some kind of magic on Charlie, Violet believed her.

Ivy pulled off her shoes then kicked them onto the mat by the door. "No. I'm sure he's just a creep. He probably just had a tarot card reading or bought a love potion at a magic shop. It's probably nothing."

"You think you would feel something like that? Doesn't seem like enough to still be hanging around." She eyed her sister for a second, then, propelled by the urge to move away from the darkened window, she started down the hall toward the staircase. She peeked around the corner toward her grandmother's room, which was dark.

"Maybe. Probably. I don't really know," Ivy said, following her up the stairs.

At the top of the stairs, Violet briefly considered taking a shower then decided it could wait until the next morning. "Where would he get something like that? A love spell, I mean."

Ivy followed Violet into her bedroom and sat on the bed while Violet kicked her shoes into her closet. "They have places. My friend Rhiannon has a shop. She doesn't sell spells per se but candles and stuff that he could burn and do his *own* spell on."

"Maybe that's what it was, then." Violet flopped on the bed and looked over at Ivy, who lay back on the bed with her head next to Violet's.

For a few moments, they lay there, staring at the ceiling together, and Violet realized she missed having moments like that with her sister. She wondered how many more they would have.

She turned to face Ivy. "You want to sleep in here tonight?"

"Clothes and all?"

"I don't care." She laughed. They were both wearing khaki shorts—not as comfy as sweats but better than jeans.

Violet jumped up to slap off the lights, but she flicked on a moon-shaped nightlight on her way back to the bed. Then they snuggled under the covers like they had when they were younger.

"The kitchen light's still on," Ivy whispered.

"I don't care." Violet giggled, suddenly giddy.

Ivy was quiet, and Violet could feel her sister's tension. *Of course he would show up just when Ivy's back.* Charlie Logan's arrival was sure to sour Ivy's thoughts of staying.

"You wanna talk about boys?" Ivy asked, mimicking a much-younger Violet.

Violet smiled then answered with the same thing Ivy always had when they were teenagers. "Sure. I'll go first."

Chapter Ten

IVY ENTERED THE BARN WARILY. She'd been there countless times in her life, and it had changed dramatically over the years. Still, after her encounter with Charlie, the place conjured a familiar tightness in her chest.

"Gran?" she called out as her eyes adjusted to the shaded interior of the building. She surveyed the white-painted shelves stocked with jars filled with jams, pickled fruits and vegetables, and popcorn kernels. She walked down the aisle between the rows of bins that would hold apples and small pumpkins in the fall. The sunlight leaking in through the red-checked curtains cast a pink glow over the humming refrigerators along the far wall. Adding electricity to the barn had been Grandpa Jack's crowning achievement, making it possible for them to store perishables. In a few months, cider would join the farm eggs on the refrigerator shelf. Selling eggs for the farmer down the road brought a little more foot traffic into the store—farm eggs were always a hot item.

At the front of the room, a black antique cash register perched on the wooden countertop. Ivy ran her fingertips over the images of chickens and trees Audrey had stenciled there. Jack had remodeled part of the barn into a store when Violet and Ivy were in grade school—not long after he'd nearly needed to bury a body there. Since then, it was where the Grants sold the fruits of their labor. The back of the barn, which held cider-making equipment, was generally off-limits to the public, though.

Despite the bright, cheery decor, which was nothing like the slatted boards and dirt floor of her memory, Ivy was ill at ease alone in the barn. Lately, the thought of being alone at all gave her the chills.

A creak from somewhere behind the counter startled her.

"Hi, Ivy," Audrey said cheerfully as she emerged from the storage area, carrying a box of empty Mason jars. A slim cat the color of golden wheat followed her, gliding gracefully around the closing door. "I thought maybe I heard somebody in here. My ears just don't work as well as they used to, though." With a clatter, she set the box on the counter. The cat settled itself on a welcome mat at the front of the counter. Its eyes closed slowly to nap in the warm, rosy sunlight.

"What's going on?" Audrey chirped. Then she took another look at her granddaughter's troubled face and her clenched hands. "What's wrong?" Her brow knitted with concern. As she came around the counter, Audrey gestured for Ivy to sit on a wooden bench along the wall. They sat together.

"I saw Charlie Logan in town last night," she said slowly. "He tried to talk to me."

Audrey stared at the floor pensively. "What did he say?" The tone of her voice told Ivy she hoped it had been merely a chance encounter.

"He told me I was pretty. And he tried to touch my hair." Ivy shivered with disgust. "He doesn't like it short," she said, touching her own hair.

Audrey took Ivy's hand and held it. She stared at their entwined hands for a moment, her forehead wrinkled in contemplation. Finally, she said, "I don't think he would come here to the farm. He's got to know that I'd make good on Grandpa Jack's promise."

"Well, I felt magic on him, and it was the same as what was in our yard after that guy was here." She waited for Audrey's reaction, but her grandmother once again shifted her gaze to the floor as if thinking.

"That's certainly strange," she muttered. "Maybe all magic that isn't ours feels the same. I can't say that I really have much experience with anything else."

Ivy didn't speak up, but she knew that not all other magic felt the same. Rhiannon's magic was very different from Violet's and Audrey's. All the magic she'd known was done with good intent, though. *Maybe all bad magic feels the same.*

"What are the odds that after all these years that you've lived here, two different people show up, stinking of magic?" Audrey let the question linger in the air as if she'd said it to no one in particular.

"I think's it's some kind of dark magic, not earth magic, Gran," Ivy said.

"There's no chance that somebody like Charlie Logan comes back with good intentions."

Audrey nodded silently just before the door burst open. The napping cat rocketed into the air, on alert.

"Hey, you've got to see this," Violet said without bothering to step into the barn.

After a glance at each other, Ivy and Audrey stood and followed.

Ivy jogged to catch up as Violet paced toward the fence near the woods. A small, swift motion caught her eye, then she recognized the shape of a brown wild rabbit.

As if she were afraid to go any closer, Violet stopped several feet away from the fencerow. She turned to Ivy and Audrey, who came to a stop next to her. Ivy nearly rushed forward to help the rabbit, which she'd thought was struggling against the foliage, pulling at something. Then she realized it was no longer struggling and hadn't been for a little while. The small creature's eyes were glazed over in death, but its muscles still twitched with unnatural motion.

"Oh, my," Audrey whispered.

"It was like this when I got to it." Violet pointed past the fencerow.

Ivy crept slowly up to the fence. Pink pasture roses were wound around the posts and creeping along the wires strung between. Just in front of the fence, several tiny brown clumps of fur dotted the grass. She crouched then jerked away as she realized that the fur was attached to entire bunnies. Some were torn apart, and others were caught in the rose thorns. Her lip curled in disgust as she looked around.

"A coyote wouldn't have done this," Violet said, her voice husky with disdain as she followed Ivy.

They surveyed the grass around them. "What do you think happened?" Ivy wiped her hands on her pants, feeling the need to clean them.

"I don't know," Violet said. "I saw one, and he looked like he was trying to pull something out of the flowers. So I came to look. But he was dead when I got here. They all were."

Carefully choosing her footing, Violet went up to the fence and peered over to the other side. She grimaced. "There's more over there."

"Did you plant these roses?" Audrey suddenly asked Violet.

A cross between confusion and irritation on her face, Violet turned to look at her grandmother. "No." Eyeing the plants suspiciously, she waved her hand over the roses. "These are wild. Besides, you hate roses—they smell like funerals. I wouldn't plant them knowing that."

Realization flashed across Violet's face, her eyes going wide. She and Audrey shared a knowing look, but Ivy didn't understand.

"What's that—"

"They're not a good omen," Violet said. "This is bad."

"Why didn't you cut them?" Ivy asked.

"I never noticed them before. It's like they grew overnight."

Then it was Ivy's turn to share a knowing look with Violet.

"He was here," they said in unison.

Audrey shook her head. "I think he's been close." She pointed to marks scratched into the fencepost. "I've put protection all around the property. And this fence is one of them. It didn't let him through. He had to stop here."

"So what happened to the rabbits?" Violet shuddered. "Did they just get caught up in it? Or did he try to send them in his place or something?"

"Do you feel anything?" Audrey asked Ivy.

All she could discern was her own disappointment over the bunnies, a few of which looked like babies. She shrugged and shook her head. "No, I don't think so."

"Then I don't think he sent them." Audrey knelt to examine the rabbit caught in the vines on the fence. "I think he was just leaking meanness, and that makes the little animals very strange."

Chapter Eleven

C HARLIE STROKED THE BOOK. HE'D made a habit of spending hours touching its pages and poring over the handwritten notes, hoping its power would wash over him. He had never really thrown in for the idea of things like magic, but the book was all the convincing he needed. It felt magical. It made *him* feel magical. The book's presence seemed to lull him into it, humming with the promise of power.

His most recent career opportunities had led him to breaking and entering, with a possible promotion to blackmailer. He had mostly gotten away with his misdeeds only because he could talk and smile his way out from under most things. But the book had changed all that.

Though most of it was written in a language neither of them understood, he and Artie had performed some of the rituals in the book, following the pictures. They'd burned a few candles, said a few chants, and brewed a few teas. And luck seemed to be coming their way. Charlie's cons went more smoothly than usual, and after stealing practically his own weight in beer, Artie had cleaned out the till at the local convenience store without so much as being noticed. So after a few weeks of practice with their new skills—and after amassing a small fortune of tens of thousands of dollars—Charlie had declared them ready for some serious magic making.

Artie had complained that they should be headed off somewhere nice or fancy with their money. However, Charlie imagined that the two of them would be like the Beverly Hillbillies if they went somewhere posh. They would stand out, and he would always feel like a fool. No, Charlie had decided that it was better to be a big fish in a little pond than any other size anywhere else. He'd headed back to the last place he had felt welcome, which was also the first place he'd ever been forced to leave. He'd come back to Oak Hill, Illinois, to see Ivy Grant.

Charlie stood just outside the door of the living room, peering in at the man sitting in the large armchair in the center. Something had gone wrong—or maybe it had worked. Charlie didn't really know the difference. But the spell had made Artie into a creature that seemed to have no need for food, sleep, or companionship beyond the ability to follow Charlie's instructions. On the outside, he still looked like Arthur Bavery, but the man inside was gone.

Charlie had never been much on responsibility, especially caring for another human being. He wasn't exactly partial to murdering his friend or leaving him for dead somewhere, either. Plus, he still thought Artie might come to be useful to him in his current state. Only, Artie didn't always carry out his deeds according to Charlie's plan, and Charlie could do little about that. At one point, Artie had spent a good portion of the day watching the wrong house. Charlie had sent the mindless goon to watch Ivy, but instead, he'd stood sentry over the neighboring house where the Grant's farmhand lived. He had remained there in a trancelike state while Charlie watched through the other man's eyes, using what the book called "a scrying pool." Charlie had stood staring at the pan full of water until his brain felt numb.

Tearing his eyes away from the silent, motionless figure in the other room, Charlie set the book down and grabbed a beer from the refrigerator. He cracked open the can and took a long swig. He pulled a pack of cigarettes from the pocket of his overshirt, which hung from the chair at the kitchen table, and stood tapping them on his palm absentmindedly for a moment. His eyes roamed the house. It wasn't new, but it was fancy. And fancy suited him. Ivy Grant suited him as well. He thought that he might like to have her house, too. The shame and jealousy that clenched his heart choked out any actual affection he felt for the girl. All he knew was that he wanted to possess her. Though he knew she'd become a woman, he found himself thinking he might have preferred the girl he remembered.

He slid a cigarette from the pack and took his beer to the other room, where his strange companion awaited him. Charlie pulled a silver lighter from the pocket of his jeans before settling into the chair in the corner of the room, his beer on the end table next to him. Then he sat in the darkness, glowering at the other man as he smoked. Artie's vacuous presence had been unnerving at first. He would often arrive silently after his tasks and go unnoticed for several moments before Charlie became uneasy under his barren stare. He never spoke, ate, or slept. Artie was so still that Charlie was barely certain he was even breathing.

Charlie cursed at the vacant figure. "You stupid son of a bitch. I don't know why I ever let you follow me around in the first place. You've been nothing but trouble for me." His cigarette crackled as he pulled the smoke deep into his lungs. Its embers glowed ominously in the dark room as it burned to the quick.

The cigarette made a vicious hiss as he dropped what remained of it into the dregs of his beer. "Artie, you might have outlasted your usefulness."

When Charlie had tried to talk to Ivy, she'd certainly seen through his charms. He suspected she just knew too much about him to be fooled. Still, he was determined to have her. Artie didn't seem to factor into that plan. After Artie's failure at the farm, Charlie had decided he would go there himself. Wired with energy after seeing Ivy, he'd been unable to sleep.

So he drove to the Grants' farm, parked his truck behind a power substation a couple of miles away from the house, and walked through the woods. At the fencerow just beyond the barn, he couldn't bring himself to go any closer—and he saw no point in turning up there in the middle of the night. That would convince no one that he'd changed his ways.

For over an hour, he'd watched the house. The kitchen light was on, but he didn't see any movement in the house the entire time he waited.

A day later, that failure continued to gnaw at him. He knew he had to do something. He no longer needed to think about Ivy's grandfather—years before, he'd seen a newspaper on his mother's kitchen table, open to Jack Grant's obituary. He was done being scared of a dead man and an old woman.

Chapter Twelve

VIOLET LET THE SEASONABLY COOL breeze wash over her as she walked the rows of the orchard. The tops of the trees rustled gently in glow of the late-afternoon sun. The far edge of the orchard gave way to a grassy path leading through the woods on the neighboring property to a large pond, the remnant of a long-forgotten strip mine, where her grandfather had taken her fishing when she was young. An aged wooden gate, half-hidden by the brambles of wild blackberries, separated the property from the Grant farm. The gate hung open wide enough for her to step through without catching her clothing on the thorny branches.

Despite the strange occurrences at the farm, she still felt safe there. Charlie Logan had certainly made Ivy uncomfortable, but if all his magic was capable of was sending a spook to watch the house and killing a few baby bunnies, he wasn't worth much concern.

As she walked through the trees, she could hear the softly lapping lake water. Dappled light reflecting off the water's ripples danced among the leaves. Violet topped a shallow round of earth that had hidden the lake from full view. She stood for a moment, remembering her grandfather. As she grew older, her real memories of him had begun to mix with often-told stories and familiar photographs. But she always remembered his eyes. Dark brown and flecked with gold, they were surrounded by deep, smiling creases in every real memory she had. Even when his voice was stern, his eyes always seemed to be hiding a secret smile. He had always been so proud of his granddaughters and everything they did, even their fantastic mistakes.

Smiling, she walked slowly, thoughtfully back to the wooden gate. She gradually became aware of the raucous calls of the blackbirds gathered in the trees. She stopped for a moment to look around. A cloud of blackbirds surrounded her, each calling to her. The urgent chorus built to deafening levels. Then suddenly, the birds fell silent. A cold chill crept along Violet's spine toward the base of her skull. She hastened her pace as she made her way along the path. At the edge of the wood, she turned to glance at the birds, who continued to watch her carefully with beady, penetrating eyes. The eerie warning that something was wrong urged her forward.

At the gate, something caught her eye. Shiny and small, it fluttered in the sunlit grass, caught on a stick just beyond the bramble wall of the dilapidated gate. Violet stooped to pluck it from the emerald-green stalks. Her fingers touched the somewhat-familiar plastic, and her mind made the connection—cellophane from a pack of cigarettes. At that very second, she heard the snick of a metal lighter case closing. She jerked upright and whirled to find Charlie Logan leaning against the fencerow, casually smoking a cigarette. The serene isolation of farm life had obviously made her complacent.

"Violet." He nodded as he flicked cigarette ashes at her feet. The smell of cigarette smoke and stale cologne caught in Violet's throat.

Her heart pounding, she backed away quickly and stumbled, barely catching herself from falling helplessly at his feet. Despite the calm demeanor, anger and menace oozed from him. Violet continued to back slowly toward the protection of her apple trees. He certainly wasn't like her memory of him. She had pictured a gangly, somewhat-aging pretty boy. This man, though, looked strong despite his wiry muscles. And his graying hair reminded her of a wolf's pelt.

"What are you doing here?" she demanded weakly.

"Just enjoying the day," he replied with a snicker. "Having yourself a nice little walk?" He flicked his nearly fresh cigarette, sending it sailing through the air, end over end, in a small, glowing arc. Though the massive stone in the gold ring on his finger glinted in the light, Violet's eyes never left his face. She grasped at the thinning rope of her composure, but she felt suddenly vulnerable in the obscured location. *If I screamed...* Violet wasn't sure who would hear. *Probably no one.* Static danced across her skin, buzzing down the backs of her legs, willing her to run. But she stood her ground.

"How's your sister doin'?" He stepped forward boldly, forcing her to back away. "Saw her in town the other night. She didn't feel like talkin', I guess."

The edges of tree branches brushed Violet's hair and shoulders, and she backed into the shade of her apple orchard. The leafy branches bent protectively around her. Charlie eyed the trees warily and hesitated at the edge of the path.

"What are you doing here?" Violet asked again.

Charlie waved toward a tackle box nestled in the grass and a fishing pole that leaned against the nearby fence. "Just doin' some fishin'. Bob's a good friend of mine," he said, referring to the neighbor who owned the property that bordered the lake. "Just doin' some fishin'," he repeated over his shoulder as he retrieved his tackle box and started through the gate. He stopped and turned slowly back to Violet. "Tell your sister I said hello."

Chapter Thirteen

CHARLIE STEPPED OFF THE LAST stair into the basement and surveyed the room. He had arranged it as the book directed, with an altar in the center. Pleased with his handiwork, he stroked the leather cover of the book he carried. It was worn completely bare around the edges so that it was a hard, shiny black.

The other people in town could never know what he kept in the house, or he would no longer be the charming stranger in town. Charlie had no desire to become the freak again. He had tried speaking to Ivy and Violet, but they were both unaffected by the magic that drew others to him. He was starting to discover that the spell had its limits: once someone managed to see past the rosy picture it painted, they seemed immune to it. A few others besides the Grant sisters had caught on. *That damn newspaper boy doesn't even come anymore.*

He had studied the book cover to cover, and he was sure he had laid out the perfect plan. He had come such a long way and made so many preparations, but Ivy Grant still did not appreciate that. *That girl will be mine yet. Time to try something bigger.* And for that, he needed a companion more useful than Artie.

After gathering his tools from the hulking steamer trunk in the corner of the basement, he laid out his things around him carefully then knelt in the center, the book in his hands. Lighting the candles, he read the incantation. Saying the words aloud filled him with an unexpected sense of power.

Thick black smoke rose from the candles and curled around him, forcing itself into his nose and throat and burning his eyes. Violent convulsions wracked his body, but the smoke continued driving into his lungs, strangling him from within. He struggled for air, unable to exhale and draw in another breath. Clutching at his neck in desperation, he fell to the ground, scattering candles and breaking the circle. A burning candle toppled to the floor but was extinguished by its own molten wax. As he lost consciousness, the other candles flickered out.

When Charlie awoke, he found himself in total darkness and disoriented. His head hurt as if he had the worst hangover he could ever imagine. His small efforts to sit up were rewarded with a piercing jolt of pain across the back of his skull. He lay motionless on the cold floor for what could have been minutes—or hours. Fatigue and darkness made measuring time impossible. For one panic-stricken second, the darkness convinced him he had been buried alive. Then his reeling mind began to recall the events of earlier in the evening... or they could have happened days ago, for all he knew. He nearly cursed himself for taking the extra precaution of blacking out the windows so that any curious neighbors wouldn't get an eyeful of his preparations in the basement.

Renewed by a sense of progress after discerning his location, he managed to pull himself to a sitting position. Then he was standing and groping for the wall, walking with his stiff arms straight out in front of him. He was farther from the wall than he had suspected. Various objects on the floor clattered as he stumbled into them. When his outstretched fingers met the cool, rough cement bricks of the basement wall, he reached up and felt for the window ledge. A few feet to his right, his fingertips scrabbled across the ledge. There, he felt for the thick, heavy curtain that he had stapled into the wood. He grasped it tightly and gave it a sharp tug. It ripped away from the staples with a rough tearing sound. A wide shaft of sunlight burst into the room. His hands flew reflexively to his eyes to shield them from the brightness.

When his eyes had adjusted, he surveyed the room. Tiny specks of dust floated in the afternoon sun that fell in a square panel of light on the floor. The markings he had made on the floor were smeared, and his tools were scattered. Someone had made quite a mess while he was out cold. Artie stood in the corner, which was no surprise. Artie often wandered silently about the house, his only intent to be near Charlie.

Rage and anger crowded out the feelings of confusion inside Charlie's aching head. He charged across the room toward Artie, whose dull, vacant eyes never even shifted as Charlie's threatening strides thumped against the concrete floor. Artie's inability to react or acknowledge the presence of another human being represented Charlie's failure. He'd rendered his eager-to-please friend into nothing but a husk, and the overwhelming need to punish someone for that failure burned into the palms of his hands.

He snatched up the front of Artie's shirt in a tight fist. With a growl, he lifted the heavy man from his feet and hurled him away with swift, ferocious power that he hadn't known he was capable of wielding. Artie's body smashed headfirst into the cement bricks of the basement wall with a dense thud and a sickening crunch, then the man crumpled into an awkward heap on the floor. Charlie went to stand over the lifeless form that had once been his only friend. The impassive eyes looked off into space, void of even the faintest glimmer of life. Charlie smiled to himself, content to have finally ended his frustration.

Chapter Fourteen

THAT NIGHT, IVY STRUGGLED TO sleep. Thoughts of her life on the farm coursed through her mind, mingling with the knowledge that Charlie Logan was nearby. A familiar vague feeling of uncertainty about the future crept in as well. Going away was an exciting prospect, but her grandmother's home was comforting and safe—at least it had been before she'd discovered the relic of a terrible memory lurking nearby.

She lay in bed, feeling the bile burn her throat and struggling to remember what had awakened her in the first place. The red glow of the digital clock on the nightstand told her that it was only 11:11 p.m. She jerked upright, throwing the covers away from her with a frustrated flourish. They had begun to smother her at some point during the last few hours, and her hair was plastered to her head with sweat. She ran her fingers through her chin-length bob, tousling it away from her head. The floorboards groaned quietly under her weight as she slid from the bed. At the window, she studied the waxing moon, still high in the cloudless sky. Her second-story room offered a perfect view of the orchard, cast in clear detail by the light of the moon. The branches of the stubby apple trees waved lightly in the gentle night breeze, making crawling shadows on the ground below.

A gray barn cat skulked across the roof of the porch, which obscured Ivy's view of the house below. The feline sprang nimbly across the open air to perch on the small square atop the nearest wooden clothesline pole. The gray cat stood silently and returned Ivy's stare for a long moment. Then the cat crossed the arms of the pole like a gymnast on a balance beam and leapt to the ground out of sight. An eerie feeling washed over Ivy like a sudden spring shower of cold water, making her shiver and propelling her into restless motion away from the window.

The house was old, like most of the houses that dotted the countryside. And like most farmhouses, every usable space was filled with something. Audrey Grant's house had extra rooms that seemed to serve no purpose other than to occupy space between the outer walls. It felt especially lonely at night. Ivy recalled how, as a child, the creaks and groans of the house would send her creeping to her sister's room for comfort. They had each had separate rooms because the house was large enough to accommodate them, but the girls had mostly lived in the same room anyway.

She crept silently down the dark, windowless hall to her sister's room. Audrey kept most of the doors in the house closed in an effort to curb the dust and the need for cleaning. The door to Violet's room was open, though. A patch of moonlight spilled through the window and out into the hall. From the doorway, Ivy could see Violet's sleeping form on top of the covers. She smiled, remembering that her twin had almost always slept above the covers in the summer, while she herself had snuggled under the blanket regardless of the heat. Ivy resisted the urge to crawl into bed with her sister for comfort again. The sort of anxiety that overcame her had nothing to do with monsters or ghosts, from which they could hide under the covers. Ivy's thoughts of her mother and her own future were specters that Violet couldn't protect her from.

She padded down the stairs, intending to make tea and selfishly hoping that her grandmother might also be awake to share in her sleepless night. However, the first floor of the house was just as dark and quiet as the second had been. She tiptoed quietly to the door of Audrey's bedroom to be sure that she was still sleeping. Only pale moonlight escaped from the space between the closed door and the wooden floorboards. Ivy stood for a moment, listening. Content that Audrey was still sleeping, she resumed her journey to the kitchen. She switched on the dim light in the vent-fan above the stove to avoid blinding herself with the brighter kitchen lights. Her grandmother's steam teakettle, in the shape of a rooster with a red comb, already sat atop one of the stove's burners. However, Ivy opened the cabinet next to the stove and pulled out the new electric teakettle that she and Violet had bought for Audrey at Christmastime. It was faster and had no whistle that would wake the house's sleepers. *I'll bet she's never even used it, either.*

She stood at the sink, facing the window, as she filled the kettle from the tap. At that moment, from the corner of her eye, she caught a glimpse of motion just outside the window. She twisted the tap, turning off the running water so she could listen. A faint rustle from the other side of the glass broke the quiet. Her breath caught in her throat. She stretched across the sink to turn off the light so that she wouldn't be visible from outside. Blinded by the darkness, she froze for a few long seconds. After holding her breath to listen, she forced herself to inhale, which seemed impossibly loud. Trapped in place, Ivy strained to hear anything out of the ordinary. Unable to decide how to react, she merely stared wide-eyed at the window above the sink. A clatter near the kitchen door sent her scurrying backward to get away from it, nearly knocking over one of the chairs. A shadow fell across the window, and glittering eyes peered back at her from outside.

"Oh, for cryin' out loud," she whispered, exhaling heavily and putting a hand over her chest to feel her pounding heartbeat. "It's the old 'cat jumps out the closet in the scary movie' routine." A fat striped tomcat balanced on the edge of the porch railing, leaning his front paws into the window's screen to inspect the action inside.

He replied in a low, scratchy meow that was muffled by the pane of glass as he pressed his whiskered nose against the screen. Looking out the window, Ivy saw that he had toppled a metal watering can in his haste to reach his perch. She had forgotten that watching the activity inside the house was a favorite pastime of the clumsy yellow cat that her sister and grandmother referred to simply as "Tom Cat." She'd been warned on her first day home not to let him in the house or they would never get him out again. He apparently wasn't a very polite houseguest. The light from the window had no doubt drawn his attention, and he was hoping for a sympathetic companion who might slip up and allow him entry.

"You might as well move along, buddy," she told the cat through the window. "I do not appreciate being snuck up on in the middle of the night. That's creepy."

Her heart was still pounding, and she was slightly out of breath. Her adrenaline had shot through the roof when the cat had appeared outside the window. She still struggled to regain her composure, peering uneasily out the window above the sink to be sure that Tom Cat had been responsible for the motion she'd seen through the glass. That window gave way to a flowerbed below rather than the porch. Ivy stood on her tiptoes and leaned against the sink to look out onto the ground. She still half expected to find something more menacing than a nosy cat.

Tom Cat called to her again, drawing her attention by thumping a paw against the screen and gripping it with his claws. Hoping he would lose interest if deprived of an audience for his antics, she went around the corner into the living room. A sweater was tossed across the back of the armchair, and she grabbed it, feeling suddenly chilly in just the small gym shorts and T-shirt she had worn to bed. She pulled her arms into the sweater and wrapped it around her tightly as she stood at the window near the front door. On the front porch stood two more cats observing her silently from the top step of the porch. A pale calico whose tail was a short nub had joined the gray female Ivy had seen scaling the roof earlier. They both scrutinized her like sentinels at a gate. The gray cat's tail twitched anxiously. The calico peered out at the yard then back at Ivy, giving her the strange impression that the cat wanted her to see something in particular. The yellow cat at the kitchen door mewled, and she jerked her head toward the sound reflexively even though the kitchen door wasn't visible from her position. When she turned back to the cats on the porch, the calico was pacing the step nervously, still watching the yard. The gray cat's attention darted back and forth between something out in the darkness and Ivy, who stood barefoot at the door.

Strange… maybe this is just what cats do. She still had not entirely readjusted to the current comings and goings of the farm life. But even if their behavior wasn't odd, it was definitely spooky. Hugging her arms tightly to her chest, she began backing away from the door. The calico cat darted from the porch, streaking toward whatever it had been watching. The gray cat turned to the yard with a low, rumbling hiss. Ivy followed the direction of the calico cat's hasty attack and locked eyes on a tall figure standing out in the grass. Too late, she realized the cats had been trying to warn her.

An ethereal voice cut the air, casting calm over Ivy. Her anxiety melted away, and the voice drew her to it. Her hand reached for the door as if she were no longer in control of her own movement. With a detached sense of wonder, she watched her hand unlatch the deadbolt and open the door. The porch's wooden floor was rough on the bottoms of her bare feet. The gray cat twined anxiously around her ankles in an apparent attempt to stop Ivy's advance into the yard. As the door coasted shut behind Ivy, the cat slipped inside. Then the door closed without a sound. The wet grass clung to her bare feet and ankles as the voice drew her forward. Hundreds of tiny, shimmering sparkles lit up the night around her, enveloping her and urging her toward a figure at the edge of the tree line.

Softly and clearly, it called out to her, "Come and take my hand. I'll take away the fear. I can set you free. Just look into my eyes."

Her vision seemed to narrow in the tiny hypnotic lights until she could only the eyes of the figure—suddenly very close and larger than life. They were the eyes of a man, the cobalt blue of a summer sky just before twilight. She had been aware of her forward motion but was surprised to find herself close enough to the man to take his outstretched hand. The pale skin of her hand shone like polished ivory under the white light of the moon and dancing lights. As she placed her hand in his, she noticed the tattoo.

Chapter Fifteen

VIOLET WAS SUDDENLY JOLTED AWAKE from her deep sleep by a heavy weight on her chest.

"Meow!" The gray barn cat stood on her chest, staring intently down at her.

"What? How did you…"

The house was stiflingly hot, and the air felt thick. Sick with the feeling that something was wrong, she cast about the room, trying to find the source of her unease. Then she heard it—a hushed, melodic voice wafted across the orchard in the small breeze. It washed over the house in waves. She jumped from the bed, her feet hitting the floor with a loud thump. She was at the window in a single long stride. She could feel a presence in the orchard. Something unwanted had entered there, and she couldn't imagine how it had gotten past her. The voice was melodic, but a sinister purpose lurked beneath the hushed tones.

She immediately spotted Ivy crossing the yard toward the group of trees. A glowing mist hovered around Ivy, shimmering and shifting as if it were alive and about to consume her. Ivy was advancing rapidly toward another figure, who was partially obscured by the branches of the trees. A sliver of clouds crossed over the full moon, blotting out the light that provided definition to the objects on the ground. *Holy hell, Ivy!*

Violet's feet pounded the wooden stairs as she rushed to wake her grandmother. She tore through the first floor of the house to where Audrey slept. She glanced out each window she passed, hoping to spot Ivy. All she caught were glimpses of the mist gathering across the yard. No Ivy. The gray cat followed right on her heels.

"Gran!" she shouted before she had reached her grandmother's door. "Something's wrong!"

When Violet burst through the doorway, Audrey was already throwing off the sheets. She snatched her glasses from the nightstand and slid them on.

"Do you hear that? Ivy's out there with it!" Violet beckoned for Audrey to follow her out into the hall. She waited only long enough for her grandmother to grab her housecoat from a hook next to the door before racing through the house.

The gray cat crouched at the threshold of the kitchen door as if watching through the crack below it. Violet grasped Audrey's hand and pulled her to it, pointing out at the trees through the door's window. They huddled together, both looking out into the shimmering, misty yard.

"What's going on?" Audrey whispered hoarsely.

The mist floated low over the grass, creating a glistening sheen on the dew-covered blades. The sight wasn't entirely unfamiliar, as the mist often accompanied the magic that Audrey worked.

"What is that sound?" Audrey asked.

"Ivy is out there," Violet answered, hearing the panicked intensity in her own voice. Her pointing finger bumped the glass. "There's something else out there, and it's making that sound." Violet strained to understand what she was hearing, but the words whispered by the rhythmic voice were impossible to comprehend. *Is it singing?*

Ivy seemed to be following the faint voice into the orchard, where its source waited under cover of the shadows.

"What is that?" Audrey whispered.

"How did it get in through the orchard, Gran?" Violet thought of the protections she and her grandmother had laid over the house over the years. "Why is she out there at this time of night, anyway?"

Audrey didn't answer.

Violet's hand was on the knob, and the door shifted under the pressure of her grasp. "Should we go out there?" she asked without taking her eyes off of her sister. Fear threatened to tear through the thin veil of her composure.

"I will." Audrey thrust her arms into her housecoat. She tied the belt, giving the knot a final, purposeful tug. Gently pushing Violet away from the door, she took the warm metal knob in her own hand. She twisted it, took a deep breath, then pulled open the door.

It brushed over the rug with a soft scraping noise. The screen-door springs gave out a small squeak as she passed through. Violet's outstretched arm caught it before it could bang on the doorframe as it closed. The muted noise seemed tremendous, but in her rational mind, she knew they were barely audible.

"Stay here unless I call for you," Audrey whispered back over her shoulder to Violet, who nodded to her through the screen.

Violet looked down at the gray cat. It looked back up at her but made no move to go outside. Out in the yard, Ivy continued to stalk across the lawn, moving unusually slowly but with intense concentration as if she were in a trance. Through the screen, a cool night breeze intertwined with the heavy summer heat.

Audrey rushed into the yard, and Violet's heart nearly jumped into her throat when she saw another figure come up behind her grandmother, just off the porch. Violet jerked open the door, unable to stand the thought of watching as something sinister destroyed the two most important people in her world. She nearly called out, then she heard Audrey's stifled gasp.

"Sam!" Audrey hissed. "What are you doing?"

Stooped as if he were trying to stay out of sight, he was clad in a pair of wrinkled, dirty jeans that must have been close at hand when he'd decided to leave the house to inspect further. His shotgun was in his hand. *Dammit, Sam. That didn't work last time.*

"What are *you* doing? What's going on out there?" he asked without taking his eyes from the figures at the edge of the trees. They were bathed in limpid moonlight and surrounded by tiny, incandescent orbs. Ivy's pale features were stark in comparison to the shadowy figure standing next to her.

"I don't know," Audrey replied as the eerie, haunting melody that filled the air grew louder. Sam began to move beyond the shadows of the house. Violet preferred to stay in the shroud, which offered a feeling of protection.

The figure turned to embrace Ivy, and the moonlight illuminated his face.

"Charlie Logan!" she said in surprise—too loudly. Audrey and Sam looked back at her, both wearing unreadable expressions.

Then Sam was moving again. Audrey gasped and clutched at Sam's sleeve, but he was far out of her reach. Charlie turned toward Sam and

Audrey with a venomous sneer. Ivy didn't move. But Sam did react. Only a few yards away from Charlie, he stopped and fired the gun. Charlie's left shoulder dipped. Violet couldn't see if Sam's shot had connected with Charlie's shoulder or not, but he appeared unharmed. Sam cocked the gun to fire again, but he was too late.

Violet watched helplessly as Charlie flew at Sam. Her grandmother raced across the wet grass. Ivy stood in silence, mystified by the action taking place in front of her.

Charlie slapped Sam's arm away. The gun flew through the air before landing somewhere in the dark grass. Sam let out a sharp cry of pain. Then another blow caught him against the side of the head, dropping him to the ground. Charlie stalked forward and grasped the older man's leg as if to drag him toward the trees.

Violet broke into a jog across the yard. Audrey shouted, startling Charlie, who jerked Sam's leg with vicious strength. Audrey shouted again and raised her right hand. A heavy gust of shimmering wind whipped away from Audrey, shoving everyone to the ground. As Violet hit the ground, the impact knocked the breath from her lungs. She found herself staring up at the starry night sky as a lone, slender cloud sliced across the moon.

Roaring with pain, Charlie reacted with inhuman speed. As Violet scrambled to her feet, Charlie whirled and grabbed Ivy. Then a flash of pale light shot through the air. Ivy and Charlie disappeared, leaving behind a faint, glimmering cloud of dust and ash that drifted down and met the dewy grass with a hiss.

"Oh my God!" came a cry from behind Violet. She spun to see Beverly racing across the yard toward her husband, her robe flapping like a cape. "Sam!" Beverly screamed.

Violet rushed to follow her to Sam's form, which was sprawled awkwardly over the grass. He was completely unconscious and bleeding from an open wound at the crown of his head and a cut just below his eye. Blood seeped from his nose and ear. The leg that Charlie had used to pull him across the ground was twisted horribly, and blood soaked through his jeans as if his leg had been torn partially away from his body. Violet choked at the thought that only the jeans were holding his leg to his torso. His arm, certainly broken, was twisted around behind his head. She slid in the grass where it was slick with blood and fell to the ground. Blood, dew, and wet grass smeared her body. She suddenly realized that she was basically naked—she hadn't worn more than her underwear and bra to bed.

She knelt next to Sam, taking an up-close view of his injuries and uncertain whether or not to touch him. "Oh, no," she whispered, afraid for Sam's life. "How did he do this?"

Sam was still breathing, but it was shallow. His injuries were far worse than she would have believed a normal man could inflict upon another with just a couple of blows. *Charlie Logan, you son of a bitch.* The thought had started to become her mantra.

Violet looked to Audrey for direction. Her grandmother's confused, wide-eyed gaze darted back and forth from a hysterical Beverly to Sam's broken body. Beverly was crying, covering her mouth and eyes with her hands as if she were afraid to look at him.

"We need an ambulance," Violet said anxiously. "I don't know if moving him would make it worse." Without giving her grandmother a chance to answer, Violet sprinted back to the house. Inside, she flicked on the lights and looked frantically around the room for the phone. Her eyes landed on her sister's bracelet lying on the counter. *Why would she take that off?* A flicker of fury ignited in Violet's gut, but it lasted only for a second before she recalled her mission.

Ivy's cell phone was lying next to the bracelet. Violet would have preferred the landline for a 9-1-1 call, but she was too flustered to recall where she might find the cordless phone. *And I just convinced Gran to get rid of the rotary phone on the wall.*

She grasped the cell phone and flipped it open. For a split second, she hesitated, unsure how they were going to explain Sam's injuries to proper authorities who knew nothing about magic. However, her concern for Sam's life overtook her need to keep their family secret intact. She punched in the numbers and waited for the excruciatingly long milliseconds between dialing the last digit and the connection.

"9-1-1. What's your emergency?"

The answer came out in a deluge of breathy words. Violet felt as if she were talking way too fast, but she couldn't slow down. She rushed across the yard as she spoke. The conversation seemed to last forever as the operator peppered Violet with questions about Sam's condition. As she stood with Beverly and Audrey, hovering over Sam, she became painfully aware of her lack of first-aid knowledge.

Chapter Sixteen

Finally, Violet heard sirens approaching in the distance. The local fire department's emergency services vehicle was the first to arrive. The EMT jumped from the vehicle, looking at Violet with confusion and suspicion, then shined a flashlight over the small cluster of the gathered inhabitants of the farm.

"It's not..." Violet looked down at her body, blankly inspecting her arms and torso. "It's not my blood." Panic clutched at her heart, stealing her breath. Her skin was slick with another person's blood. Tears of panic welled in her eyes. Turning away from the EMT, she doubled over, gasping for air. The emergency vehicle's flashing lights shrank to tiny pinpoints in her vision. She heard the arrival of another ambulance, followed by hurried, insistent shouting.

The EMT draped a blanket over Violet's shoulders before guiding her over to the truck and sitting her inside. "It's okay. Just take deep breaths, slowly."

Violet pulled in ragged breaths, but she was regaining her composure. She watched as medics dressed in blue uniforms loaded Sam, who was already on a stretcher, into the back of the second ambulance.

"Can I get dressed?" she asked the female EMT. "I feel like half the town's about to see me in my underwear." Violet tried to smile weakly, but it turned into more of a grimace.

"This was not an accident, right?"

Violet shook her head. "No."

"Then maybe you should just stay wrapped up until the police talk to you. I don't know if they'll want to make a record of any of that stuff on you or not." Her shoulders hitched toward her ears in apology. "I'm sorry.

I don't know the rules about that stuff, and this is a really weird scene. So just to be sure. Okay?"

"Okay." Violet nodded. Nothing on her body was going to give them any clues about what had gone on there, but pitching an argument would probably raise suspicion.

A county police patrol car pulled up, and Kevin jumped out, slamming its door behind him. His panicked eyes scanned the scene, and when they found Violet, he stalked across the lawn toward her. The EMT stood protectively next to Violet. *Oh, great...*

"Are you okay?" Kevin asked, his voice strained.

Violet nodded, drawing the blanket tighter around herself. "Yeah. They're taking Sam." She pointed toward the ambulance as it pulled away.

He turned to look in the direction of the retreating ambulance. More flashing lights appeared in the distance, signaling the imminent arrival of more police.

"And he took Ivy." Her voice was thick with checked emotion. She swallowed hard, pushing back tears.

"Shit, they said there was an intruder. I thought maybe you were..." He reached out to touch her, but he faltered as his eyes traveled to her body then to the EMT, who was watching him intently. "Whose blood is that?" he asked, locking eyes with the EMT.

The woman cocked her head, motioning for him to step away and speak with her. He followed her around the front of the truck, into the headlights, folding his arms across his chest.

Violet leaned forward so she could see them. The woman pointed out things in the yard, including where Audrey still stood, absentmindedly staring at the trees. Kevin looked at Violet through the windshield glass and shook his head. His lips shaped the words "just the blanket" before he looked away. The EMT nodded and slid a chart off the hood of the truck. Kevin flipped through the pages then scribbled something on one of them. Then he turned and jogged toward the arriving police cars.

"He said that he just needs the blanket and what you're wearing if it has all of the stuff on it," the EMT said to Violet when she returned. "We can go to the house to get clothes if you want. He'll talk to you after." She smiled at Violet.

"Thanks." Violet looked over at Audrey, who was pointing toward the trees as she spoke to two officers. Satisfied that Audrey was okay, Violet led the EMT into the house.

In the kitchen, the other woman stopped short, blinking at the dirty, bloody partial footprint on the rug at the door and the smeared blood on the kitchen table where Violet had retrieved Ivy's phone. Violet's gaze followed hers, and the reality of the situation hit her in another unyielding wave. Her breath caught in her throat with a squeak, and tears escaped her eyes. She wiped them away hastily.

"It's okay," the other woman said to Violet. "They'll find her, and your neighbor's in good hands."

As she stared at her own bloody handprint, Violet said quietly, "He'd better not hurt her."

In the bathroom, Violet turned on the shower then stripped and handed everything to the EMT through the partially closed door. She rinsed briefly in the ice-cold water. Still shaking from adrenaline and chilly water, she wiped away any lingering debris with the towel on the rack. Shuffling movement and talking filled the hall—more people had entered the house. She pulled denim shorts and a wrinkled YMCA T-shirt from the laundry hamper and dressed as fast as she could.

Outside the door, Audrey and a man Violet instantly recognized as the county sheriff had replaced the female EMT. Audrey immediately pulled Violet into her arms and hugged her tightly.

"Your grandmother says that this man took Ivy with him," Sheriff Carl Owens said. The sheriff had lived in the area nearly his entire life, and he had a reputation as an honest, dedicated peace officer—and the first black man ever elected to the post.

Violet disengaged from her grandmother's grip to face him. "Yeah, I saw her with him in the yard, and I went to wake Gran. And then Sam was shouting, and he had a gun. Gran and I went outside, then he jumped at Sam. And Sam just crumpled." Violet's face twisted in reaction to the memory.

"It's okay," Sheriff Owens said, his tone soft. He had a kind face, but it didn't hide the hint of suspicion that glittered in his dark eyes. Violet searched her grandmother's expression for clues about how to react.

"Who had the gun?" Sheriff Owens pulled a notepad from his breast pocket.

"Sam did. Sam was hurt, and Bev screamed, and then he was just gone, and so was Ivy." Seeing the muscles in Audrey's neck tighten, Violet stopped speaking.

He leaned in closer to her. "And that's all?"

Violet nodded. "I ran over to Sam and slipped in the grass." Her stomach lurched, and she took a deep breath. She looked up at the ceiling and let her breath escape in a slow hiss, trying to regain her composure. "I called 9-1-1, and it was kind of a blur after that."

"Did you recognize the man?"

"I think… I think it might have been Charlie Logan." Violet knew for sure it'd been Charlie, but she was uncertain about whether or not to tell the sheriff. "He, uh, kind of has a thing for Ivy, and he's been here before."

The sheriff nodded. "Your grandma said that he used to work here." His practiced and comforting tone conveyed his attention without being patronizing. But his raised eyebrows and searching gaze betrayed him—he did not believe that Charlie Logan posed any danger to Ivy. "Do you think it's possible she left with him willingly? You said he didn't come into the house. Did your sister ever mention a relationship with a man? Do you think he could have injured Sam in self-defense?"

Violet understood the warning in her grandmother's eyes. Charlie seemed to have everyone in the town spellbound, able to see only good in him. She'd seen it in at the grocery store, and Ivy had described seeing the same at the strawberry festival. "Um…" Violet chose her words carefully. "I didn't say that he didn't hurt her. Maybe Gran said it—she was closer, after all. I've always found him… unsettling, and I really don't think that Ivy had a relationship with him. And he's shown up here uninvited at least once." Despite attempts to mask her frustration, Violet's voice was strained. "And Sam's never made a habit of shooting at people on our property." She quickly amended her statement, remembering that he'd recently told the police different himself. "He probably always has his gun ready, but he's never shot at anyone. And we seem to have had our share of strange visitors lately." Violet's chest tightened, but she forced herself to remain still. She hadn't really allowed the reality of the situation to fully sink in. She knew she would lose control if she did. *Sheriff Owens probably thinks I'm nuts.*

"Okay. Well, Sam and Bev are on the way to the hospital. They'll take good care of him there, I'm sure." His eyes searched Violet's features. "We'll have someone stay until morning, and we'll probably be back to look at more things then. We'll get looking for Ivy right away."

The sheriff stepped back so that he could look at both Audrey and Violet. He seemed more intent on protecting the man they had accused than finding Ivy.

Audrey pulled Violet close, hugging her around the waist with one arm.

"Ladies, I really think we're going to have her back safe and sound real soon. Just let us know if you think of anything else that might be helpful." He gave Audrey's shoulder an encouraging squeeze and turned to leave.

"Thanks," Audrey called after him.

He gave her a little wave as he closed the door behind him.

Chapter Seventeen

"So he thinks we're big, fat liars," Violet said after he'd gone. "Everyone in town thinks Charlie is wonderful—and for no apparent reason. He's really obviously creepy, don't you think? Or at least the stereotypical creepy?"

"It's my fault," Audrey said quietly, staring at the floor. "I should have dealt with him for good the first time." She hugged Violet again, clinging to her remaining granddaughter. They stood together like that until the squeak of the screen door in the kitchen interrupted them.

They turned to face Kevin Bonniere. He was rubbing his palms together nervously, seeming uncertain about where to stand. His jaw was tight and determined, but his concern was evident in his eyes. "Something strange is going on here. This is not how we usually do things. Your sister is basically missing—kidnapped—and Sam was severely injured by an intruder…" He put his hands on his hips. "Everyone else just kind of wandered off. Did Sheriff Owens even talk to you?"

"Yes," Audrey said from behind Violet. "But he seemed to think that Ivy just decided to leave on her own."

"And you don't think so?" Kevin turned to glance out the door.

"No," Violet and Audrey said in unison.

"Of course not. I saw how she looked when she saw that guy the other night. And what the hell happened to Sam?" He jabbed his thumb toward the door. "That's not the sort of scene where we just assume everyone's fine and a grown woman took off with her boyfriend."

"It's a spell." Audrey jerked open a cabinet drawer, rifled through it, then pulled out a tarnished brass key.

"A *what?*" Kevin asked, his eyes wide, as Audrey turned and hurried down the hall to her bedroom.

"He cast a spell to comfort everyone or at least fog their minds. I've read about this before. I'll find it…"

Kevin and Violet followed her voice, which trailed her down the hall. In her room, Audrey was kneeling in front of the chest at the foot of her bed. The lid creaked as she lifted it.

"I know where she is," Violet said, suddenly struck with the thought. "I know exactly where he is." She turned to Kevin. "We need your help. He's the one in Libby Walsh's house—he has to be." She turned back to Audrey. "He must have a ward on it. No one around town wants to talk about it. Have you noticed? And I even started to go there one day and just got distracted on my way over."

"Wait. What?" Kevin asked again. "A spell? Are you ladies talking about magic here?"

"Yes," Violet answered. "I don't really have time to explain it now, but yeah… magic." For some reason, he hadn't been affected the same way everyone else seemed to have been, but she was too grateful for his presence to delve into why he was unaffected.

Audrey slowly closed the lid to the trunk and tucked the key into her pocket. "It doesn't work on us because we're stronger than he is." She gestured toward Kevin. "He's got a protection spell of some sort on him," she told Violet as she stood up.

"Huh?" Kevin's eyes were wide when Violet turned to look at him. He shrugged and shook his head slightly. "Maybe… I-I dunno. How would I know?"

"Okay, doesn't matter right now." Violet put a hand on his arm. "We need to get Ivy right now."

"Okay. So where's this Libby Walsh live? I've heard the name, but I don't know her." Kevin took off for the kitchen door with a purposeful stride. "I can at least go over there and see who's around. Maybe I can get Sheriff Owens back over there if I find something. There's certainly something strange happening here. None of this feels right." Hand on the doorknob, he tilted his head toward the yard. "Nobody out there was following procedure. And these are not people who don't know how to do the job."

I knew I liked this guy for a reason. Violet followed him. "I don't think she lives there anymore. No one seems to quite know where she moved to, either." She turned to scribble a crude map on a used envelope then handed it to him. For a second, her hand hovered over Ivy's bracelet lying on the table, then she snatched it up and loosened the cord. "Take this, too."

He held out his open hand, but she folded his fingers into a fist and slid the bracelet onto his wrist. His hand felt so warm in hers, and her ears burned with shame that she'd had that thought when she had more important things to handle. *Head in the game, Vi!*

He nodded slowly. She wasn't sure if his lack of questions meant he understood or that he simply thought she was too crazy for any of it to matter.

"You stay here. I'll give you a call as soon as I know anything," he said.

"He's scary, okay? For real. Be careful." She looked back at her grandmother for confirmation.

"And try not to touch him," Audrey added.

Kevin nodded.

He was halfway down the porch steps when Violet grabbed Ivy's car keys from the counter. She turned to find her grandmother standing in the hall, holding a shotgun.

"We're going, too," Audrey said.

"Yeah." Violet nodded.

As soon as Violet turned the key in Ivy's car, loud music filled the interior. "Holy shit!"

Audrey jerked forward and turned it off then settled back into the seat, staring blankly ahead. "It might have been easier if he'd just gone off with the others, Vi."

That thought had already occurred to Violet—she'd managed to put everyone she cared about in the path of a supernatural steamroller. Violet sped through the night, refusing to agree aloud. Only the choruses of the frogs that lived in the ditches broke the silence. She followed Kevin's car at a distance, hoping not to be noticed, though he probably knew they were behind him anyway.

At the end of the street where Violet was sure Charlie lived, Audrey instructed Violet to turn off the headlights as they followed the squad car. The house sat at the edge of town on a particularly large lot. That meant it sat farther away from the neighboring houses than most of the others did. The fenced-in yard gave way to a field, where the corn was already knee-high. The pointed leaves of the stalks rustled slowly and stiffly in the night breeze. The road was paved as far as the house's drive, but it gave way to a dirt path only a few hundred feet beyond the edge of the property. The grass was slightly overgrown as if the lawn had been neglected.

The silver halo of dawn was just beginning to form. In the half-light, a trellis and arbor heavy with climbing roses that had grown into unruly brambles cast strange shadows across the side yard. The house looked surprisingly unkempt, considering that Charlie couldn't have been there for more than a few months.

Several yards from the house, Violet cut the engine, and the car rolled toward the house with only the sound of the tires crunching on blacktop to give them away. When it came to a stop, Violet and Audrey slouched in their seats.

Kevin was already out of his vehicle and approaching the house. From their vantage point on the street, the house looked dark and silent. Kevin moved toward the front door, his hand on his holstered gun.

It's fine. He does this all the time. It's his job.

"How in the hell did this happen?" Audrey whispered without taking her eyes off the house. "This whole place is a terrible mess. He was *here* the whole time. Even the yard is trying to destroy that house because he's doing evil magic in there."

"Don't know, Gran. I think that's why the neighbors haven't noticed, either." Violet turned to scrutinize the emotions flooding her grandmother's face. Then Kevin's voice made her turn back to the porch, where he was standing.

"Marshall County Police," he stated loudly as he rapped on the metal screen door. Then he rang the doorbell, which was illuminated by a tiny light within itself. "I'd like to talk to you, Mr. Logan." He jammed the doorbell a few more times in rapid succession. The front door had no window, and he leaned over, trying to see inside the window next to the door. Though Violet couldn't see from her position, it must have been blocked by curtains, because he made no further effort to look through the window. He rang the doorbell again. "Mr. Logan! Are you home?" he shouted into the closed door.

One hand still on his gun, he pulled open the screen door with the other. He leaned in and pounded on the wooden storm door with his free hand, then he grasped the doorknob and shook it. Violet guessed it was locked—he stepped back to close the screen door.

To her horror, the door flung open. Then something swooped out and dragged him inside the house. A muffled cry followed in his wake.

Chapter Eighteen

"WHAT WAS THAT?" VIOLET SHRIEKED.

"Shhhh…" Audrey hissed back, motioning for Violet to be quiet.

Violet's hand was already on her the car door latch, and she popped it open.

"Wait, wait!" Audrey grabbed Violet's arm. Then she reached into the floorboards behind the driver's seat and withdrew the shotgun.

Violet's eyes widened with uncertainty about her grandmother's experience wielding the weapon. She hadn't objected to her grandmother bringing it along, but she wasn't sure about actually taking it out of the car. Grandpa Jack had taught his granddaughters—not his wife—how to shoot.

"Okay, now go." Audrey nodded for Violet to exit the car.

Here's hoping I don't get shot. She slipped out quietly without completely closing the door behind her, and Audrey followed with the gun. They both hurried across the front yard, toward the row of lilacs that blocked the view of the backyard. Staying low, Violet jogged through the tall grass. After pushing between two bushes, she made room for Audrey to follow. The older woman worked her way through the growth, keeping the barrel of the gun pointed at the ground. Without speaking, they made the mutual decision to go around the back of the house rather than confronting the main entrance.

The secluded backyard reflected the same disuse and poor maintenance that the front yard did. Mrs. Walsh had always kept the house tidy and in good repair. But weeds had sprouted from the gutters, and the siding on the house seemed to be molding. *I can't believe no one noticed this. Then again, I didn't even drive past.*

A small sliver of flickering yellow light escaped the basement window near the ground. She scrambled to her hands and knees in the wet grass to look inside, ignoring the pebbles and mulch digging into her knees. With her eye to the slit in the heavy cloth that covered most of the window, she could see parts of the room below. Quiet shuffling sounds and whispered conversation filtered through the glass partition.

Feeling her grandmother's breath on the back of her neck, Violet struggled to piece together the glimpses of light and movement inside. Then she caught sight of her sister's red hair.

Pointing urgently at the glass, she shifted away from the slit, and Audrey moved into her spot and craned her neck to peer through the crevice.

"Ivy," Audrey whispered.

Violet leaned away from the window and cupped her hand around her grandmother's ear. "We've got to get in there."

Audrey stared silently into the window. Something crossed the space between the curtain and Ivy's hair. Audrey and Violet both jerked back.

Audrey nodded. "Yeah, somebody's in there."

Heavy steps retreated from their hidden point of view, and the basement fell silent.

"He went upstairs," Violet guessed.

Audrey leaned forward and pressed her ear against the glass as if that might give her a clue about Charlie's whereabouts.

"Can I break the window?" Violet asked.

Audrey looked up and down the house, and Violet followed her gaze to a cellar door a few feet away, obscured by grass and weeds. She wondered if it was rotting as rapidly as everything else seemed to be.

Audrey pointed to the cellar door. "No, not the window. Break that."

They crouched at the edge of the door. The tassels of overgrown crab grass brushed Violet's legs and elbows. Audrey held the shotgun across her knees as she studied the door, which suffered from a serious case of dry rot. The padlock was caked with brown rust. Violet gingerly reached out for the lock then shook it lightly to see how well it was affixed to the door—no sign of budging. But its equally rusty hinges looked less sturdy.

Violet motioned for her grandmother to back away from the door. "I'm going to kick it." She searched the wood for a weak spot. "There." The corroded hinge near the bottom of the door looked loose.

"You can't just kick it. Are you crazy?" Audrey whispered. "You'll either make too much noise or break your leg off."

Violet shook her head silently. Time was passing too quickly, chasing headlong after a conclusion she couldn't stomach. If Charlie had left the room, he wouldn't be gone long—and Ivy wasn't the only one in that house with that lunatic. Violet didn't know when the police would arrive or even if they were on the way. Kevin might not have believed her when she'd told him Charlie was dangerous. So maybe he hadn't even called anyone else before going to the house.

"I think he's waiting for sunrise, anyway. That's when the magic is the strongest." Audrey waved a hand in a gesture that encompassed the house. "Look at this house. It's falling down and rotting. The natural world outside the house has to be weakening his dark magic. He probably can't do it until the magic peaks, or not here anyway."

Violet surveyed the surroundings. Vines tangled with loosened shutters, and moss pressed itself into crevices in the siding. Her grandmother was right about the magic, but she didn't agree that they could count on Charlie to wait for sunrise. He might save Ivy for sunrise, but Charlie didn't have any magical purpose for Kevin.

She looked down at the work boots she had pulled on before leaving the house. They were heavy enough to bust the wood.

"I've got to break it," she whispered. A knot of urgent energy pressed against her stomach, squeezing her ribcage. She jumped to her full height and lunged forward, and her right foot struck the door just below the battered hinge. As the corner of the door gave way, her momentum carried her forward, and she lost her balance. Both hinges creaked and peeled away from the doorframe. Without a solid barrier to stop her foot, her body went down along with the door, her bare leg dragging across rough wooden boards as her foot descended into the dark basement without the rest of her. The top of the door, freed from its shackling hinges, rushed up from the doorway to knock her backward. As she fell, she clutched at the door to keep it from banging loudly back onto the doorframe.

"Unnnn…" she grunted as the pain shot up her leg. *Wish I'd worn pants instead of shorts,* she thought as she lay under the door, her left leg bent awkwardly beneath her and her right leg halfway into the door opening.

She struggled to free herself without losing her precarious grip on the door's rotten wooden edge.

"Dammit, I told you not to do that!" Audrey clamped her jaws shut as if she were forcing herself to be quiet.

"How else did you expect me to break it, anyway?"

Without answering, Audrey fumbled with the shotgun and finally laid it down beside her before reaching out to help Violet lower the door quietly.

"It always worked better on *Charlie's Angels*, huh?" Violet said over the pain.

"Yeah, it did. Now, get the hell out of there." Her arms under Violet's armpits, Audrey pulled her granddaughter from the hole.

Violet grimaced as her leg dragged against the wood in a new, and equally painful, direction. She looked down. In the dim light, she could see that she wasn't bleeding. The scratches were just deep enough to burn but not bleed. It would hurt like hell later, but the adrenaline pumped away that pain for the time being.

The women shifted the door again so that they had room to descend the steps below it. Audrey took a deep breath. Then she took a few steps into the hole, crouching on the steps just outside the pool of light cast by the basement lighting. Violet followed. She pulled the door back over the opening as best she could, hoping to conceal their entry into the basement in case anyone came into the backyard.

The cellar steps gave way to a dark corner of the basement where the light didn't quite reach past the stacked boxes that lined the floor next to the stairs, creating a fort from which Violet and Audrey could observe the rest of the space. As Violet peeked over the stacks and turned to survey the room, Audrey grabbed her face lightly, forcing her to meet her gaze. With her other hand, she pointed to the adjacent corner of the room then made a shushing gesture with her index finger over her lips. Violet nodded then swiveled her head to look. Her eyes went wide and her breath caught in her throat when she saw what had drawn Audrey's attention.

The heavy-set man who had been standing in their pumpkin patch in the rain lay crumpled in a gruesome pile against the wall. Half sitting, his body looked as though he had hit the wall flat on his back and slid down to the floor. Wide-open eyes stared at her, but the irises and pupils were clouded over with a white, filmy haze. His sallow features hung slack from his face. She thought he was wearing the same clothes he'd been wearing the day she had seen him. *That was weeks ago. Could he have been dead that long?* He certainly didn't seem to have decayed enough for that to be the case. Violet was no expert on these matters, but she did watch enough cop shows on television to have gathered a little knowledge on the subject.

She tore her eyes away from the gory scene, and her gaze fell on her sister. Ivy was sitting in a wooden chair that looked as if it had long ago been a part of an expensive dining set. A large braided rope tied around her arms and torso held her loosely to the chair, which started out wide at the top and tapered near the seat. A smaller rope encircled each of her wrists, which lay in her lap. Her eyes were vacant and her face serene.

Violet started to move toward her sister, but a shuffling sound at the top of the stairs stopped her. She and Audrey froze, stooped in the shadows like rabbits hoping to hide in plain sight if only they could be still enough. Footsteps descended the basement stairs, and each was followed by a light thump. Then a figure emerged into the stairway opening. Violet found herself staring at Charlie, but his physique had changed. At the bottom of the stairs, he stooped to avoid banging his head into the top of the door opening. Moving with a heavy gait, he entered the basement like a wild, prehistoric creature stalking its prey.

Though still human, Charlie merely *resembled* the person he had been before. He seemed larger, and his skin seemed waxy and taut as if it could barely contain his menace, which threatened to overflow and tear him apart at any moment. The familiar face was distorted by a frantic sneer. His once-blue eyes were dark, nearly black.

Violet forced herself to breathe slowly and quietly. Her nostrils flared as she tried to suck oxygen from the musty basement air and instead drew in faint traces of paraffin and smoke mingled with the smells of dust and mildew. Panic gripped her chest when she managed to drag her eyes from Charlie's ominous presence to the shadows behind him. She suddenly understood the faint thumping sound that had followed each of his steps as he descended from the darkness into the lit room.

Clutched in Charlie's hand was the collar of a jacket—a brown jacket with the word *Police* across it in yellow letters. He was dragging an unconscious Kevin Bonniere down the steps behind him. The soles of Kevin's shoes hit the basement floor with a slap. The sound was followed by the swish of his pants sliding across the smooth cement. Charlie lowered the other man's head slowly to the floor near the chair holding Ivy. Numb with fear and indecision, Violet wanted to run to them, but she recalled how quickly Charlie had snatched Kevin from the front porch. And flashing memories of Sam's thick blood reminded her how swiftly Charlie had ripped apart the older man. The fright overtook her need to rush into action. She reached behind herself, groping for Audrey.

Chapter Nineteen

AUDREY TWITCHED WITH TENSION. As Violet squeezed her arm, Audrey felt her chest tighten, and she wondered if she was having a heart attack. Maybe a lack of blood flow had brought on some sort of hallucination. She closed her eyes tightly and breathed quietly and slowly. When she opened her eyes, the scene remained unchanged. In that second of determination, she realized the gun was no longer in her hand. It was lying in the grass near the cellar door. *Dammit!*

The monster that occupied Charlie Logan's body stretched upward to its full height, dwarfing everything else in the room. His large frame seemed to absorb the light around him. As he lifted his face to smell the air like a dog sniffing the wind, a snarling smile twisted across his features.

Terror coiled itself into a ball inside Audrey's stomach.

"Ahh… Violet… Audrey, you've come to join us?" the Charlie monster asked patronizingly as he looked around the dimly lit room. His voice was thick and low as if his throat were coated in syrup. "'Come into my parlor,' said the spider to the fly…" He threw his head back and cackled at his own wicked joke. The laugh crackled through the air like static on a bad radio station.

"Oh, shit!" Violet whispered loudly, shrinking behind the stack of boxes that shielded them from his view.

Audrey clamped her hand over Violet's mouth. She wasn't certain that he knew *where* they were, only that he knew they were close.

"I have your man, and I have your girl," Charlie crooned in a mocking, singsong voice. His eyes were carefully scanning the room. He squinted into the dark corners. Audrey and Violet peered through the small slits framed with cardboard.

"Quietly, quietly," he hissed. His eyes moved past Audrey's hiding place then slowly returned and settled there. "Quietly, quietly, we're hiding, aren't we? I see you, though."

Audrey's grip tightened on Violet's face and arm. Even if she and Violet could get out, she had no idea what he would do to Ivy. Unable to bear the thought of losing both girls on the same night, she wanted Violet to be somewhere safe, far from the dark place. Violet's tension hummed beneath Audrey's hands. The girl was like a crouching jungle cat ready to spring. Violet was a kinetic creature, always drawn into motion. Her quiet contemplation was almost always followed by violent, aggressive action when she was cornered. And they were most definitely cornered at that moment.

"What are you doing with Ivy?" Audrey called out from behind the boxes, hoping to stall long enough to push her terror down so she could think clearly again.

The Charlie creature smiled, seeming pleased that his suspicions were verified. "Charlie always liked this one. He set me free, gave me form. So I wanted him to have her." He stroked Ivy's hair softly, like a possessive child with a favorite doll.

Ivy blinked slowly, still dazed.

"I like her, too. She's… lovely." He laughed again, and the sound sent chills down Audrey's spine.

"You're not Charlie. What is your name?" she asked quietly. Her terror had blossomed into blind panic, but her voice remained even. *I should have realized sooner*. He wasn't a man anymore. Something heinous and horrible was only pretending to be Charlie.

Another menacing laugh split the air. "I have no *name*," he shouted, his amusement replaced by sudden anger. Ivy's eyelids fluttered, then she blinked hard as if struggling to wake from a deep sleep. Her eyes moved to Charlie, and she jerked in the chair, flinching away from him. The wooden chair legs squeaked on the smooth cement floor with the startled movement, but Charlie paid her no attention.

"I come from the dark places in the hearts of men, where they are afraid to say they have dared to look. I am not deserving of even a name!" he shrieked and shook his fists in the air. His skin seemed to squirm over his muscles as though his anger threatened to burst out of the skin that contained it—held it at bay from punishing the world. He stalked forward with newly intensified hatred.

Ivy's eyes went wide with fear. Audrey realized the monster must be losing his control over Ivy if she was lucid enough to be afraid. Audrey wondered if his concentration was failing along with his composure.

Audrey shrank back from the wall of flimsy cardboard, letting Violet slip from her grasp. She looked at Violet, whose eyes were locked on the basement floor where Kevin lay. He was no longer limp. The visible tension in his body told her that he was conscious but trying to avoid notice. When the monster moved away from him, Kevin's eyes fluttered open to take in his surroundings.

Charlie crossed the long room in fewer strides than Audrey had expected, and Kevin pulled himself into a sitting position next to Ivy's chair. Ivy was breathing heavily—she was no longer calm and dazed. She struggled against the rope that pinned her arms loosely to her waist, wriggling it toward her shoulders. When Kevin touched the ropes, she panicked, tipping the chair. For an agonizing second, it teetered as Kevin grabbed for the chair back—then it clattered to the floor. *No!*

With a wild roar, Charlie whirled toward them and raised his hand as if he intended to strike Ivy. The rubber soles of Kevin's shoes squeaked softly on the slick floor as lunged forward to shield her with his body. In that confused, startled moment, Violet's tight muscles uncoiled and launched her over the boxes onto Charlie's shoulders.

"No!" Audrey cried helplessly as the toppled boxes knocked her into the block wall. Her head smacked into something hard, and a flash of light and pain split her vision. She pressed a palm to her temple.

Clawing at the creature's eyes, Violet dug the heels of her boots into the hollow spot at the base of his sternum. He loosed a pain-filled howl. Reaching back, he caught her by the back of her shirt then flung her head over heels. She hit the floor and slid into a stack of old books, collapsing it. A rack of coats toppled over her.

Dark smoke wafted from gashes in Charlie's face below his right eye. "He never liked you, you little bitch!" he roared at Violet.

Then he unleashed another scream as he knocked Kevin away. Charlie clutched at Ivy, who was trying to force the rope past her shoulder and over the back of the chair without choking herself, but it was too wide. Like a turtle balanced on its shell, Ivy was terrified, exposed, and unable to escape.

Charlie grasped her bound arms and started to pull her to him, the rope taut against her throat. Then Kevin fired his pistol. Grinning, Charlie looked down at his torso. More dark smoke bled from the tear in his white T-shirt.

"What the hell *are* you?" Kevin cried in a voice tinged with panic and frustration. Another deafening shot rang out, hitting Charlie without any apparent effect.

A twisted smile spread across Charlie's face. "I had a use for you, but you aren't as smart as I thought." He grabbed Ivy's chair and pulled it to his side with his left hand as if it weighed no more than doll furniture and she were a doll. Then he reached for Kevin with his free hand. His eyes flashed red.

Violet's voice cut the air in the room. "You don't get to have her no matter what the hell you are!" Kicking at the coats clinging to her ankles, she stumbled forward. Her anger and hatred uncoiled from her body in a ball of light. A clap of thunder accompanied the sudden, howling wind that rocked the house and banged the cellar door.

Wind rushed into the basement, swirling dust and scattered items around the room. The writhing ball of light encircling Violet ripped away from her body and knocked Charlie to the floor. A peal of thunder shook the foundation of the house as the fluorescent lights tucked into the ceiling of the basement sizzled and popped. In the darkness, Charlie yelped like a wounded animal.

Violet shouted unintelligible words of anger again, accompanied by a roar. Another flash of lightning revealed the room for only a second. Then Charlie's shirt burst into white-hot blue flames, and he screamed in pain. The smell of burnt ozone cut the air. He pushed Kevin aside as he fled up the stairs. Before the light of Charlie's burning body diminished, Audrey saw Violet sink to her knees. Then the room succumbed to darkness.

After a few quiet heartbeats, Ivy screamed suddenly, an astonished, confused cry that sounded as if it had started deep inside her core. Audrey heard a faint click, and the narrow shaft of a flashlight beam exposed the wreckage within the darkened room. Kevin, holding the flashlight, turned for the stairs then winced and let out a hiss as he clutched at his stomach.

Surrounded by scattered books and clothes, Violet went from a kneeling position to all fours as if her energy had been drained from her. The ripped neck of her T-shirt revealed red marks that promised to darken into purple bruises along the back of her neck and shoulder. Matching marks dotted her arms, and scrapes and shallow scratches crisscrossed her right leg. Still, she shook her shoulders back and raced for the stairs.

Ivy was crying softly as she finally pulled her hands free from the braided ropes holding her wrists together, but the second rope still pinned her to the chair. Patching together the jumbled, broken chain of her thoughts, Audrey willed her body to move. She wobbled uneasily toward her granddaughter. Kevin looked as dizzy as she felt, but he handed her the flashlight and a pocketknife then trudged up the stairs after Violet.

Chapter Twenty

A<small>T THE TOP OF THE</small> stairs, Violet jerked to a stop at the sight of Sheriff Owens standing just inside the back door, pointing a gun right at her. "Get down!" he ordered.

Reeling, Violet dropped to the floor and scrambled to put her back against the wall next to the stairwell just as the sheriff fired. Behind where she'd just stood, Charlie's hulking figure panted, still alight in white-hot blue flames. Then he roared and charged toward the sheriff. His eyes shone like a wild animal's in the night, reflecting the light of the breaking dawn.

Charlie barreled past Sheriff Owens, knocking him into a recliner. As he smashed through the glass storm door, he tore the screen door from its hinges. A wailing wind followed him through the doorway, and static electricity prickled Violet's skin once again.

"Holy hell!" Sheriff Owens shouted from beneath the toppled chair.

The scuffle of someone ascending the stairs in a hurry made Violet hesitate for just a second too long. She followed the sound of a wounded howl through the broken back door. Her boots crunched shattered glass on the back porch.

In the silver glow of morning that streaked the dark sky, she saw Charlie crouch and take to all fours like a dog. Bulbous drops of rain began to fall. A harsh hiss like the sound of water on a campfire followed Charlie across the grass, through the broken fence, and into the field of corn just beyond the yard.

Violet jogged to a slow stop in the grass, knowing she didn't have the energy to chase him and that she would lose track of him right away in the field of corn. The sound of her grandmother calling her name drew her attention back to the house. Lights were on in a few of the neighboring houses. Confirming her suspicion that at least one of them had already called the police, an approaching siren wailed.

"Shit!" she whispered, wondering how she and Audrey were going to explain the situation to the sheriff and the neighbors. She cast one more hesitant glance over her shoulder, toward the cornrows, and walked back to the house.

Stepping through the smashed glass door and into the house, she found Sheriff Owens and Ivy kneeling next to Audrey, who was sitting at the top of the basement steps, holding her head. Her eyes were squeezed shut in pain. Kevin was standing but hunched over, leaning on the upended recliner. *Well, aren't we a pitiful lot.*

"I think she's going to need to go to the hospital," Sheriff Owens said to Violet as she dropped to her knees clumsily next to her grandmother. He looked Violet up and down. "I'm pretty sure she's got at least a concussion. And from the looks of it, Bonniere might, too."

Violet looked up at Kevin, who avoided her eyes by looking out the window. The sound of the siren grew closer.

"But first, I'm going to need somebody to tell me what the hell that thing was, preferably before that cruiser gets here." He looked at Kevin expectantly.

"I don't know, Sheriff," he said. "Charlie Logan, I guess."

The sheriff pulled a disbelieving face. "That was not a man. That was…" He rubbed his temples then shrugged. "Where did he go?" He looked over at Violet.

"He's gone. Out in the field." She attempted to point, but her arm just sort of flopped in the direction of the door.

In the semidark, the sheriff locked eyes with Kevin. Then he turned to the women. "All right, ladies, here's the thing. I am not going to be able to put into a report that I showed up here on a whim and found my deputy along with you three, then I shot at a wild man-animal who looked to be on fire, but there wasn't any fire." He shook his head.

Violet hadn't considered what the rest of the police department, let alone a town full of people who would hear the story secondhand from Charlie's neighbors, would think of the sheriff—or Kevin.

"They won't believe you," Audrey said, not looking up.

"No, they won't." His gaze moved from Kevin to Violet. "So for now, you tell everyone Kevin and I agreed to come here after leaving your house, and you two followed." He waved a finger from Violet to Audrey. "Without my permission," he added with jab of the same finger. "Logan had Ivy in the basement and claimed to have a weapon, which I suspect he used to injure Sam back at the farm. We each fired during a scuffle, then he fled."

"We're going to lie on the report?" Kevin asked.

"Yeah," Sheriff Owens answered with a perfect poker face.

"I think that's probably a good idea," Kevin said.

The sheriff didn't look around to see if anyone else agreed. He patted Audrey's shoulder as he stood. "We'll get you an ambulance here ASAP." He flicked a light switch, but the lights didn't even flicker. "That lightning must have hit the house earlier."

Violet knew she was responsible for the outage, but the sheriff's explanation was more believable than hers.

"What made you come?" Kevin asked the sheriff. "I couldn't get you on the radio, or—"

"We'll talk about that later." Sheriff Owens opened the front door and started to step out. "I think you did good, though. You did the right thing. Don't worry. I'll take care of it."

The flash of blue lights lit the room as a cruiser pulled up in front of the house. The responding officer met the sheriff on the porch, exchanged a few words with him, then jogged back to his car.

Sheriff Owens poked his head back inside. "Do you think there's anyone else in the house, Bonniere?"

"No, Sheriff."

He nodded. "Then, Miss Grant, I'd like you to accompany me when we look through the house while Kevin and your grandmother go to the hospital. There're some things here that I want you to explain."

"Okay." Violet stood.

"And after that, I think you need to get looked over, too," the sheriff said.

"I'm fine."

"You look hurt," Kevin said, his eyes suddenly soft.

"And you're *definitely* hurt, Bonniere," the sheriff said. "Mrs. Grant needs to see a doctor, and Ivy seems shaken up right now, so she can give her official statement at the hospital. Violet and I will follow you to the hospital before long."

"Oh, wait, Sheriff." Kevin raised his arm and winced. "Dammit. Um, there's a dead guy in the basement."

"Okay. That should go in the report."

Ivy had spent the entire conversation sitting quietly next to Audrey, holding her hand. Audrey whispered to her, "Tell them he hit you in the head to get you here."

"Is that what happened?" the sheriff asked quietly as his officer returned to the house.

Ivy shrugged limply. "I don't know. I don't remember leaving the house. I just remember the cat…" She grimaced and shrugged again.

"You should probably just say that then. Sounds like a head injury." He turned to his officer outside as Audrey and Ivy exchanged a look of uncertainty.

Things had spiraled way out of control, and Violet was inclined to let the sheriff handle things. *We couldn't possibly go to jail for this.* She wracked her brain for illegal activity. *Well, there was the breaking and entering.*

"The ambulance is here, Sheriff. Reynolds will meet them at the hospital."

"Okay, and have dispatch put in a call to the coroner's office." Sheriff Owens shook his head. "We've got a body in the basement."

Once the ambulance had gone, two uniformed officers arrived and did a check of the house before leading Sheriff Owens back through with Violet in tow. In the basement, the dead man was still slumped against the wall, but everything seemed strangely innocent in the morning light filtering through the busted cellar door.

"Someone will be back to take photos," Sheriff Owens explained to Violet after she told him the man was already dead when she and Audrey had arrived.

"There's a shotgun outside the cellar door. It's Gran's," she told him quietly. "I'm sure she has a permit and everything. If not, I've got a Firearm Owners ID."

He nodded. "That's fine."

The first story of the house seemed somewhat lived-in, though it could have used a good dusting. However, the second story smelled stale and unused.

One of the officers pushed open the door to a bedroom. "This is how we found her," he said to Sheriff Owens.

Violet hadn't been to the upstairs and wasn't certain why the sheriff still needed her. Confused, she leaned around the sheriff to peer into the room. A swift stream of chilled air rushed into the hall despite the humidity in the rest of the house. The air inside the room was several degrees colder even though the power had been out for about an hour by then. No one had asked yet why it was out, and Violet didn't offer to explain.

In an overstuffed recliner facing the window-unit air conditioner, Libby Walsh's body was slowly mummifying. The side of her face closest to the air conditioning unit was dry and cracking. The sheriff swallowed his disgust in a heavy gulp. A silk scarf hung limply around her neck as she sat looking out into the backyard. Violet didn't detect the stench of rotting flesh, and she wondered why. She realized that the body in the basement hadn't decayed, either. *What the hell was he doing here?*

"He was living here with two dead bodies?" the officer asked.

"Looks that way," Owens answered.

"For how long?"

"A while, I'd say. That's the coroner's business."

The sheriff excused himself and Violet as more officers descended on the house. He walked her to one of the patrol cars and opened the door for her. When she was inside, Sheriff Owens reached across the seat to turn on the engine. "Wait here."

With a nod, she let him close the door then watched him speak briefly with a man who'd stepped out of a hearse belonging to the local funeral home. The coroner, she presumed. After shaking hands with the funeral director, the sheriff walked toward the car. He stopped for a moment, studying the overgrown yard. Turning slowly back toward his vehicle, he put a hand to his chin and rubbed it down his neck, deep in thought. Violet tried to prepare herself for being alone with him but didn't know what to expect. He seemed to be taking all the strange events in stride—everyone seemed to be handling the situation well, in fact.

For a heartbeat, she imagined Kevin's face after Charlie had escaped. He'd seen things she was certain he didn't understand, but he was still concerned about her, as if he still cared about her. Violet shook off her thoughts of Kevin as Sheriff Owens got into the car.

He sat motionless for several heartbeats, staring straight ahead, his hands on the steering wheel. Then he took a deep breath, as if he'd finished processing the thoughts he'd saved for that quiet moment, and put the car into gear.

"I'm sorry I didn't listen to your grandmother before. I just... I know she's a good lady, and I should have at least checked on this guy." His demeanor had certainly changed, as if a spell had been broken. He was no longer the skeptical and dismissive Sheriff Owens he'd been hours before.

An apology was the last thing Violet had expected to hear. "I think Charlie Logan had everybody fooled. He was always a little like that."

"So how dangerous is this? I have a feeling something bigger than I can imagine is going on, and you ladies seem to be at the center of it."

"I don't really know where he's been since then, but he used to work for my grandpa. He... well, he behaved inappropriately toward Ivy, and Grandpa ran him off."

Sheriff Owens looked at her out of the corner of his eye. "You mean he assaulted her?"

"He *would* have, but no, he didn't."

"Okay." He nodded slowly, absorbing the information before moving on. "Okay, then why is he... not a person anymore?"

Violet tucked her hands into her lap. "I can't really answer that. Sorry." She looked at the man, whose dark hair sparkled with silver at the temples. The creases at the corners of his eyes made him seem trustworthy. And he'd lied so far only to protect her family. She decided to go for broke and trust him with everything. "I don't really know for sure, but I think he cast a spell on himself that went wrong. I think maybe that's what happened to the guy in the basement, too. I also think that's how he stole Ivy and was strong enough to tear Sam apart like that—I think he used magic."

"That house was a wreck. I mean, it was half fallen down on the outside. I don't know how I've been driving past that house every day on my way to work without noticing how terrible the yard looked, all grown over like that. I just... I didn't see it until we came back out. And I couldn't even say where I thought Libby was. Poor woman. If Bonniere hadn't accused me of not doing my job if I didn't go..."

"I think that was magic, too. He kept people from noticing. But once you did notice, you couldn't stop noticing. I doubt any magic is absolute." *I can't believe he hasn't called me crazy yet. Even I'm not sure I'm not crazy.* Magic was one thing—monsters were quite another.

"I didn't know a person could do such a thing…" He couldn't seem to finish the statement or meet her gaze.

"I don't know how to do that, if that's what you're thinking."

They rode in silence while Violet worried that she should have kept her mouth shut and let her grandmother decide what to tell the sheriff. He stared ahead at the road, gripping the steering wheel with white-knuckled hands.

Without looking over at her, Sheriff Owens finally answered, "I think that… man was the scariest thing I've ever seen. I do not want that walking around my town, where my children live. Do you know how to stop him? I mean, do you know about *magic*?" He said the last word as if he felt silly saying it aloud, as though he might be admitting he believed in fairies.

"I don't know anything about that stuff he was doing. Gran might know. All I know for sure is that he wanted Ivy for a reason. He's always had a thing for her."

"Kevin said he shot him, and it didn't even faze him."

Her heart sank a little when she thought of Charlie looming over Kevin. "Yeah, that happened."

Sheriff Owens pulled into a parking space near the emergency entrance to the hospital then turned in his seat to face Violet. "I'll come by the house to visit your grandmother and ask her about this. For now, we tell no one about what we talked about in this car. If an officer named Reynolds comes to talk to you in the hospital—and he probably has already talked to the others—stick to the story we talked about at the house. We'll deal with the rest later. I get the feeling the usual police procedure isn't going to do us any good with this thing."

His tone was so sincere that Violet had the feeling he wanted to add, "I'm not a bad cop, I swear."

She shook her head. "I don't know much about police procedure, but it's probably not going to help much."

The sheriff walked Violet to the emergency room check-in. "I'll talk to you both later. Oh, and I'll have someone bring the Cavalier over to the hospital."

"Thanks, I would appreciate it."

He gave her a smile and a nod before leaving her to talk with the receptionist.

Chapter Twenty-One

SPORTING A FRESH BANDAGE ON her leg, Violet moved quickly and quietly down the empty hall toward Kevin's ER room. The ER doctor had poked and prodded her until he was satisfied that her injuries were entirely superficial, then the nurse had slathered her with ointment and bandaged her up.

She peered around the doorframe to see if Kevin was alone. He sat at the edge of the bed, pulling on a T-shirt over his head very slowly. His lean, muscular frame suddenly seemed gaunt and fragile. A large red mark stretched from the top of his bellybutton to just below his right nipple. Violet winced when she realized that it was the shape of a hand—a slightly singed and misshapen handprint. His head appeared through the neck of the shirt, revealing a patch of shaved hair over his left ear, where a row of butterfly tape stitched together a long cut, tracing a sickeningly reddish bruise that spread from his eyebrow to his hairline.

His eyes met hers, and a wave of self-consciousness washed over her. He'd seen her secret: the angry electricity. Guilt immediately followed—she'd convinced him to go to that house.

"Come in. Close the door."

She slipped into the small, windowless room and softly closed the door behind her. Uncertain where to stand, Violet leaned against the door, still holding the doorknob behind her back. The look in his eyes told her not to come any closer.

"Did you talk to Sheriff already?" he asked, his voice hard.

"Yes," she answered. "And Jeff Reynolds."

"Yeah." Kevin nodded. "He was here, too. What did you tell him?"

"I told him that we followed you and Sheriff Owens to the house, and

Gran and I broke the cellar door and got involved in the scuffle. Charlie said he was armed, so you fired. The lights went out when that quick storm hit, and Charlie ran upstairs." She raked still-messy hair away from her face with her fingers. "Sheriff Owens told me to stick to what he said at the house. Gran had some tests—or is having some tests—on her head... so I don't think she has talked to anybody yet."

"That's not what happened," Kevin said tersely. He frowned, a mix of confusion and frustration darkening his features.

"Did you tell him what happened? Reynolds, I mean," Violet asked gingerly. *Did you lie for me?* Things had moved beyond her control, but she wasn't sure if he knew they were beyond his. She'd given up control to Sheriff Owens, but had Kevin?

She waited for him to speak, though she wanted to touch him, reassure him, ask him to reassure her—anything other than wait.

"I told Reynolds that Logan hit me"—he gestured to the cut above his eyebrow—"and then dragged me to the basement. Then the rest of what Sheriff said."

Violet let a sigh of relief squeeze out of her—partly because she didn't want to have to explain the reality to anyone else and partly because she didn't want to be the only one who'd lied to an investigator. She remained stock-still, pressed against the door.

"I had nothing for why there was a dead guy in the basement already or why you were there." His eyes were glued to Violet's face, searching for the answers to his questions. "That's what Sheriff Owens told me to say... for now."

"I'm sorry," she said quietly.

"What the hell *was* that, Violet?" He spread his arms in front of him in a gesture of sheer bewilderment. "I have never seen anything like that. I know Sheriff saw something he couldn't explain, or he wouldn't have told us to lie."

"Would you believe that it was an electrical fire from the lightning?" she asked without meeting his gaze.

He closed his eyes and rubbed his brow with his thumb and forefinger. "Not even a little. But I meant that guy... that *thing*." The muscles in his jaw flexed as he struggled to put his thoughts into words. "Your grandma talked to him like she knew what was going on." He looked up at her, almost pleading for her to offer a realistic explanation—even if it was a lie. "I took your word on going to that house. Did you know that guy could knock my head in, and I wouldn't be able to do a damn thing?"

Violet moved toward the bed hesitantly. "I knew he was a bad guy, but I didn't know he was *that* dangerous or that your gun wouldn't work. I told you to be careful, but I… Sam's older, and you're… I didn't know what else to do. I didn't really think you would believe me and go over there. And a little bit of me wanted me to be wrong about him." She reached out to touch Kevin's cheekbone below his black eye.

Turning his head slightly so she could inspect his wound, he let her touch him. When her fingertips met his skin, his muscles tightened, reminding her of a wild animal submitting uncertainly to another, more dangerous animal.

Another wave of guilt washed over her. "I'm so sorry you got hurt. I would take it back if I could. I wanted to as soon as you left my house. That's why we came."

Suddenly, he grabbed her wrist and pulled it away from his face. He turned her hand to inspect her palm. "What was that thing you did in the basement? With the light." He turned his gaze to her face. "I think you might have saved my life."

Violet felt her pulse against her skin where he touched her. That same heartbeat was cacophonous against her eardrums, drowning out her thoughts and her attempts to find the right answer. She stood mutely, unable to flee from the direct confrontation. Answers and their consequences whirled through her mind, not a single one slowing down long enough for her to catch it. She started to back away, but Kevin tugged her closer so that she leaned stiffly against his shoulder, bracing herself for rejection.

"Look… uh… people talk, you know." He scrunched his eyes and shook his head slightly, and Violet knew the words hadn't sounded how he'd wanted them to. "I always thought it was just rumors. It doesn't matter. They said stuff about me and mine, too."

"I didn't really know people knew," Violet said quietly. *I'm so stupid. Thinking we could keep a secret. Not in this small town.* For the first time, she understood how Ivy felt—floodlit and overwhelmed by the possibility of judgment. Their mother had sealed them into that fate when she'd left her children behind.

Heat crept up her neck to her temples. The sudden urge to move, to be away from Kevin, coursed through her. She twisted away from him, and he reached out to stop her, but halfway through the motion, he winced and cradled his side.

"Hey, wait. That's not..." He kept his voice quiet as if he knew she wouldn't listen anyway.

To her relief, he didn't follow. That would only draw attention from hospital staff and other patients, which would make things worse. She forced her feet to walk slowly until she rounded a corner into a hallway where four vending machines stood. Trying to sooth herself with the comfort of a small, secluded space, she stood between the vending machine and the corner of the hallway. She squatted, balancing on the balls of her feet, and took deep breaths. Feelings of insecurity washed over her, forcing her to recall her every action in a new, ugly light. She was exposed—and apparently always had been. As the waves of anxiety ebbed, Violet told herself that nothing had changed. Half the town probably thought whatever they'd heard was rumor. The other half probably wouldn't have liked her regardless of the secrets her family kept—if she could even think of them as secrets anymore. *You don't mind being the subject of rumors, remember?*

Anger at her mother for abandoning her and Ivy flared up inside her. That anger raged whenever Violet's anxiety surfaced. She liked to believe that no one would have paid them so much attention if Rachel hadn't taken off, leaving a mystery in her wake. The mood didn't last long—it never did—and she composed herself. She shook it off and left her hiding place.

Violet found her sister in her grandmother's hospital room. Ivy was curled up next to Audrey on the bed, her knees hugged tightly to her chest. Audrey was staring out the window, with a vacant look on her face. The rain had given way to a sunny morning with vivid blue skies.

"Well, this was not a good night for the Grants," Audrey said, keeping her gaze trained on the window. "Gayle Sweeny was Sam's nurse when they brought him in. She said that they Life Flighted him to Saint John's." She turned to face Violet. Her face was tight, and tears glittered in her eyes. "Gayle said they didn't really think he was going to be okay. He lost a lot of blood, and there was a lot of damage. The ER doctor kept asking if he'd been caught in a tractor PTO or a sweep auger. Sheriff Owens said he didn't really know if the doctor believed that Sam just had a scuffle with some guy in the yard. It looked a lot worse than that."

Violet's heart sank as she realized just how badly things had gone over the past evening. She'd been concerned about what people would think after the rumors of what happened at Charlie's house started to fly, but she'd forgotten that meanwhile, Bev was alone in some visitors' lounge, waiting to find out if her husband would live or die. Her grandmother seemed to have aged years in the last hour. Ivy looked small and frightened. Violet swayed a little. Her head felt heavy, as if its weight would topple her to the floor.

Audrey waved her over to the chair beside the bed. "Sit down, Vi. You look a little peaked."

Violet crossed the room and eased into the chair. With fingers soft and comforting, Audrey brushed back the loose hair from Violet's shoulders to look at the bruises across her neck and shoulders.

"I'm sorry, Violet," she whispered. "I should have known. I should have seen it sooner." A cluster of tears spilled from Audrey's eyes and wove their way through pinched creases in her tight face.

"Oh, Gran," Violet said quietly. "I don't know how you could have— how any of us could. We just… didn't know." She rubbed her face. Her skin felt hot beneath her frozen hands. "We can't help what Charlie did. I don't know how you could have possibly guessed he would turn into that. In my whole life, I've never seen anyone else's magic. Who would have thought Charlie Logan, of all people, would show up like that? We did what we could."

"You did good, Violet." Audrey petted Violet's hair.

A few moments later, a doctor in scrubs knocked on the open door then entered, flipping through pages on a clipboard, a second clipboard tucked under his arm. "Hello, Mrs. Grant," he said to Audrey before turning to Violet and holding out his hand. His eyes flickered to the bandage on her leg, but he didn't ask. "Dr. Harris."

With a nod, Violet shook his hand. "Violet."

"Well, I think you're going to be fine, Mrs. Grant. We'll let you check out today. I don't see any reason to keep you here—unless you're not feeling well. Any blurry vision, headache, that sort of thing?"

"No, sir. My body feels well enough."

Ivy stirred and sat up, blinking hard and looking up at the doctor. "Sorry, I fell asleep."

"You're fine, dear." Audrey patted Ivy's hand.

Dr. Harris smiled briefly then returned his attention to the chart again. He scribbled as he spoke. "So I'm going to mark down that your scans were fine. I do think you hit your head pretty hard, but I wouldn't expect any lingering effects. If you feel dizzy or really tired or emotional in the next few days, you need to come back here or call your primary care physician. I'll make a note that your regular doctor should follow up in a week or so." He looked up and smiled at Audrey. "I think you're going to be fine, though. The nurse will probably come by in few minutes to get you ready to check out." He pulled the second clipboard from under his arm. "And it says here that Ivy Grant—"

"That's me," Ivy said quietly.

Dr. Harris smiled and nodded. "Well, we don't need to do any tests for your head. So you're ready to go home as well. Just take it easy if you're feeling rundown."

"Thank you, Dr. Harris," Audrey answered.

Chapter Twenty-Two

J UST AS THE GRANDFATHER CLOCK struck five o'clock, Violet heard a knock at the door. She answered it to find Kevin waiting on the porch. Freshly showered and shaved, he still looked a little worse for the wear. He was leaning sideways against the doorframe, scanning the orchard through squinted eyelids.

"Hello?"

Kevin turned, offering her a tight smile. "Hey, I, uh, wanted to apologize about earlier."

Violet's face scrunched involuntarily. *I almost got him killed, and he's here to apologize to me?* Realizing she was snarling at him, she relaxed her face, but the rest of her body wouldn't cooperate. "For what?"

"For the hospital. I was trying to say thank you for saving my life, and I ruined it." He stepped closer, and the smell of his soap wafted over her.

"Look, if you don't want anything to do with me anymore, it's probably—"

"No," he said quietly, running a hand lightly down her arm. "I don't understand... I just... can you tell me what that was? Has that happened before?"

After Violet had driven them home from the hospital that morning, Ivy had gulped down a sleep-inducing tea and gone to bed. Violet suspected Audrey had also fallen asleep.

"Do you want to come inside?" She stepped back and motioned for him to enter.

"Sure." He hesitated on the doorstep.

"It's fine. We're not vampires or anything." She turned and went to the kitchen, expecting him to follow.

He stopped at the table, gripping the back of a chair. "Jesus, Violet. I do not know what to say here. I imagine the proper way to handle something like this is to give you space or something then ask you out on a date again—or for the first time, maybe. But I don't think we have that kind of time." The muscles in his arms flexed as he squeezed the chair even tighter. "That thing was scary, and it's still out there. Is it going to come back here? For your sister? For *you*?"

Violet's heart melted just a little at the soft tone in his voice. "I don't know where to start." Her tense posture wilted.

"I know what it feels like to be different," Kevin said.

"You don't, not really," Violet answered. "You said it yourself—people talk. We're probably a novelty at Halloween. People come to the farm and buy their pumpkins from the witches. I got used to it, and it's easy to forget, I guess. Or sometimes, I think the attention is because we don't have actual parents."

"My dad was a mean drunk, and my mom left without a word when I was ten years old. You think *you* get fake sympathy, you should come back to my hometown with me sometime. It's like half of them think she's terrible for leaving her kid with a man like that, and the other half think maybe she's…"

"Buried in the backyard?" Violet finished.

"Yeah." Kevin nodded.

"Where do you suppose these people think my mother is?" Violet asked with a fine edge of anger in her voice.

"I don't care much what people think, really," he told her with sincerity-filled eyes. "You think you're a freak or something, but I think you're beautiful. Those people do, too. That's why they stare." He reached for her hand. "Look, I like you, Violet. I don't know if I've made that clear. I just… I'm not good at that."

Violet looked down, wanting desperately for this man to be telling her the truth. She'd fooled herself for so long that she just wasn't interested in romance, but deep down, she knew that wasn't the entire truth. Her fear of being rejected because she was different kept her from getting too close to people. Sometimes, she thought she could just hide away on the farm for the rest of her life.

Knowing she'd allowed Kevin to witness the magical part of her life made Violet want to run away. Though never "popular," she'd always had plenty of friends. However, she'd never told a single one about what her grandmother had taught her and Ivy. She'd talked about her missing mother but kept the magic closer to the vest.

"Look, when I saw the… magic, that wasn't what scared me," Kevin said. "That's fine. My mom was gone, and my grandma took care of me a lot. She didn't do magic like that, but she believed." He blinked hard and shook his head a little. "I didn't. I should have, but I didn't. And that thing… was…" He locked eyes with Violet. "Scary as hell. I would believe in anything after seeing that."

"Okay, but everybody else isn't you. And they didn't see it."

"Sheriff Owens saw it, Violet. He's willing to listen, and he's not going to go telling people anything like that. If he does, he'll look crazy, too. He's an elected official. He can't afford to look crazy."

She plucked up her courage, and wanton fearlessness filled her. *I already told the sheriff, anyway.* "It's magic, like spells and brews and standing over a cauldron… we're basically witches, Kevin. But it's not like in the movies— we don't have a coven, it's nothing to do with the devil, and I don't really know where it comes from. That's the truth." A bit of relief washed over her when he didn't stop her or look terrified. "It's been passed down through my grandmother's family for generations, and we're just made that way. My mother… well, I don't know where she is. No one seems to know. And I don't think that has anything to do with witchcraft. She's just one of those moms."

"Do you know other witches?" he asked tentatively. "I mean, what happened to Charlie? He did that to himself? Is he a witch?"

"I've never met anybody besides Gran and Ivy who can do what we do. And I don't know who did that to Charlie. He *must* have done it to himself. I've never seen anything like that. For us, magic is mostly making plants and things grow."

"Your grandmother knows how it happened, though, don't you think?"

Violet furrowed her brow. "I just can't believe none of this is that weird to you," she said, not answering his question.

He produced an oblong stone from his pocket and held it out for her inspection. Shades of brown and cream swirled on the surface of the smooth, polished rock. "Your grandmother said it herself—somebody already put a spell on me." He pushed to rock closer to her. "This is it, I think. I'm telling you—my grandma believed. She told me never to go anywhere without this."

Violet recognized the stone's magic, and she felt the rock's vibration even before she reached for it. When her fingertips touched the smooth agate, the vibrations buzzed against her own, and a small spark jumped from the stone as if it had been struck against flint. A small smile quirked the corner of her mouth, and she looked up at Kevin.

"Yeah, Violet, I'm not scared of you. I just need to know how to protect you from that monster. I'm a man with a gun, but what am I supposed to do if I can't use it?"

A knock at the door interrupted them. Kevin pocketed his stone without saying another word, and Violet went to answer the door.

A somber-faced Sheriff Owens was standing outside, holding open the screen door. Under one arm, he carried an opaque blue plastic bag. Even though sunglasses shielded most of the dark circles under his eyes, he clearly hadn't slept in the hours since he'd dropped her off at the hospital. Violet didn't know what to say, so she only smiled politely.

"I need to talk to you ladies," he said, shoving his sunglasses up into his hair.

"Sure, come in." She backed away to give him room to enter. "Gran and Ivy are both in bed for now." She pointed a thumb over her shoulder toward her grandmother's bedroom. "They were pretty shot after last night."

"Not you, though, huh?" He eyed her closely.

"I'm not really partial to the idea of having us all take a nap while Charlie Logan is still out there."

"Wise girl." He looked around the house as if he were taking in every detail and storing it for future recollection. Her eyes followed his gaze around the room, but she didn't recognize anything that should be important to him. "I talked to Bonniere after he left the hospital today. He said he was coming to talk to you."

"Oh." She nodded. "He's in the kitchen."

The sheriff followed her into the kitchen. He nodded at Kevin, who returned a knowing glance. "Look, I think that this Logan person was a bad guy. I don't think any of you did anything wrong, but I've got two dead bodies in that house and a whole load of things I can't explain... I don't exactly want to send my guys looking into it without me knowing what's really going on." He rubbed his hand over the dark stubble on his chin. "And I need your help to find this guy before he hurts someone else." Finally meeting Violet's gaze, he said, "And I have something I want your grandmother to take a look at." The sincerity in his eyes washed away the last of her doubts about him.

"You can sit down if you like, and I'll go check to see if Gran is up." She gestured toward the kitchen chair.

"Thanks." He set the blue bag on the table and pulled back the chair with a squeak.

Down the hall, Violet eased open the door to Audrey's room. Her grandmother stood in front of her dressing table, hastily running a brush through her hair.

"I suppose that's the sheriff at the door?"

"Yes, he has more questions about last night. He wants to know what's going on before anyone else does. Oh, and he has something he wants you to look at."

Audrey straightened. "Well, let's go."

Chapter Twenty-Three

AUDREY FOLLOWED HER GRANDDAUGHTER TO the kitchen, preparing for a conversation she had hoped she would never need to have. It had arrived: the day she would have to explain herself to the world outside her family. The sheriff didn't seem the kind of man who would gossip. However, years of feeling self-conscious about her family's state of affairs had made her gun-shy.

The sheriff waited at the table, his chin propped up against his fist, staring into the wood grain of the tabletop while Kevin Bonniere stood quietly, leaning against the counter. They both seemed separately lost in thought, though they were probably considering the same thing.

Sheriff Owens stood when Audrey entered. "Mrs. Grant," he said with a nod.

"Hello, Sheriff Owens." A blue bag on the table caught her attention.

"I suppose I'll just get to it. Violet told me a little about Charlie Logan, but there seems to be more to it than all that."

Audrey told the sheriff how Charlie Logan had been a relative of a relative of Jack's, and Jack had given him a job on the farm. "Then Jack told him to leave after he caught Charlie cornering Ivy in the barn. I should have noticed the way he always watched her…" She swallowed the painful lump in her throat. "I don't know how he came to know enough about magic—or anything else—to be capable of the mess he's made. I never really thought he was all that smart—or industrious." She pointed to the bag. "That's got something to do with it, though."

She couldn't tell for sure what was in the bag, but Audrey could feel a fey and malevolent energy emanating from the object inside. It was magic—dark magic. She'd known it existed but had never actually felt it until she stepped foot in Libby Walsh's house the night before.

Ivy wandered into the room, rubbing a hand over tired eyes. "What's going on?"

"The sheriff wanted to ask a few things about Charlie." Audrey noted the way that Ivy's eyes locked onto the bag as if she couldn't look away.

Ivy peered over Audrey's shoulder. "What's that?"

The others moved forward as the sheriff pulled a leather book from the bag. Ivy physically recoiled at the sight of it. Violet perched on a chair next to her grandmother.

The old leather book was worn shiny and smooth at the edges. Though a tight strap held the pages inside, many were loose and stuck out from the cover at odd angles. The creases in the loose pages looked new. The book had obviously been cared for over the years, but its most recent owner had not taken such pains to preserve it.

"We didn't really find much at the house—nothing we weren't expecting to find, anyway. Charlie Logan had definitely been living in that house for weeks, or months maybe. We found an ID for the man in the basement. His name was Arthur Bavery. He had family in the area, but he wasn't a local. And we found a bunch of candles and things—occult stuff that we didn't know what to do with. I've called in the state police to do forensics since there's a murder, but—and I hope I've done the right thing here—I took this before the evidence was cataloged. Given the nature of the crime and this piece of evidence, I thought you ladies might know more about it than a bunch of police, even the 'experts.'"

Evil resided in the book, and Audrey was wary of touching it. Still, she reached forward gingerly and turned to a page marked unceremoniously with a piece of a used envelope. The book was old, and the pages were dark with age, but the envelope was new.

The page bore handwritten notes in a mix of English and a language that Audrey did not recognize. She flipped a few pages and scanned the writing—still more words that she didn't understand. Small parchment pouches shaped like envelopes had been sewn into the heavy pages. The others stood around her in rapt silence as she returned to the marked pages. One of the small envelopes there was marked with a word she did recognize. She suddenly realized what the book was.

Ivy leaned forward to point at the writing along the top of the page. "It's a bokor zombi spell."

"A what?" the sheriff asked. "A zombie spell?"

"Like *Day of the Dead*?" Kevin asked.

"No," Ivy said, shaking her head. "Like voodoo."

"This whole book is a collection of spells and potions," Audrey said.

Violet flopped back in the chair, crossing her arms over her chest. Audrey suspected the others didn't notice her granddaughter's hard, knowing glance. Charlie had most certainly used magic he hadn't understood.

"This envelope is datura powder." Ivy pointed to the pouch. Then she gestured toward the word *vodou* at the top of the page. "A *bokor* is a voodoo priest, and they use this to put a person into a death-like trance. According to the tradition, when the person wakes up, they're under the bokor's power. Depending on who you talk to, the zombi is either a reanimated corpse or a live person under a sort of hypnosis." Ivy was suddenly full of information, and Audrey had no idea where she would have gathered it.

"The guy in the yard who was dead in the basement…" A glimmer of recognition flitted across Violet's eyes.

"Yeah, probably," Ivy answered.

"How do you know this?" the sheriff asked, echoing Audrey's thoughts. He looked at Ivy with narrow, suspicious eyes. Violet and Audrey also turned to her questioningly. Kevin stood apart from them, still avoiding meeting anyone's eyes.

"I know some people in the city who know a lot of stuff about the occult." She bent over the book. "They call this a book of shadows. The spells aren't the kind of thing I would try to do or anything. I don't know why anyone would want to, but I find it interesting, and I read and talk to people." She shrugged as if to pass off her knowledge as a mere interest, but Audrey could tell it was more than that.

"Okay. What about the guy in the yard?" Sheriff Owens asked, looking from Ivy to Violet.

"They called about a weird guy watching the house a few days ago," Kevin chimed in. "I answered the call, but he took off before I got here."

"It was the same guy," Violet finished.

"If they were friends or working together, that explains the other guy," Sheriff Owens said, regarding the book with a wide-eyed stare. "But what about that thing inside of Charlie Logan?" He turned to Audrey. "What was that? Did he find it in that book?"

"Well, I'll show you what I think it is." She rose from her chair. "I have a book in the other room."

He nodded to her as if to give her permission.

Chapter Twenty-Four

I VY SAT NEXT TO VIOLET as Sheriff Owens's gaze followed their grandmother down the hall. They waited in silence, staring uneasily at the book. Kevin moved forward as if to touch the book, then he halted abruptly. Violet gently took his hand and moved it away from the pages, concern in her eyes.

"I was just going to see if there's anything useful, but—" He stopped himself as if uncertain how to finish. Ivy knew he was feeling the book's evil aura, whether he realized it or not.

"I wouldn't touch it." Violet shook her head slightly. "There's something wrong with it."

They all looked back at the book in expectation of something awful.

"What kind of skin do you think that is?" Kevin asked quietly.

The sheriff sat back, making a sound in his throat that told Ivy he'd just swallowed a little bile. "How about the language? Do you know what language that is?"

"Gullah or Creole probably." Ivy leaned forward, just a little bit, to study the writing. "I don't know, really."

"I would say it's Creole," Kevin said. "Some of my mom's family speak Louisiana Creole. Looks like that."

The sheriff looked expectantly at Kevin.

"I don't read it or anything. I just see a few words that look familiar."

Audrey returned with her own book, which was also old. The shape of a tree was pressed into its leather cover. Heavy leather thongs held it together at the spine.

"This is my family's book of spells," she said as she laid it out. Both girls looked at her inquisitively.

Ivy had suspected her grandmother had a book like that. Rhiannon had a book of spells, as did each of her Wiccan acquaintances, though theirs tended to look more like crafty scrapbooks than Audrey's did.

"I've never showed this to the girls," Gran told the sheriff without looking at Violet or Ivy. "My family's ancestors have gathered together their knowledge of the natural magic and spirits they've encountered for generations. That's how the girls and I know these things—it's our family's history." She left the explanation unclear, and Ivy wondered if the sheriff even wanted to know more than that.

She flipped through the yellowed parchment pages. Some of them, mixed in with the others, looked much newer as if they had been added to the book at different times. The turning pages slowed, then they stopped as Audrey found the page she was looking for. She turned it so that Ivy could see. As Violet stood, a look of indignation broke through her obvious attempts to hide it.

"I think this is what's inside Charlie." Audrey pointed to a pencil drawing of a dark smudge with eyes drawn in red ink in the center. "It's an evil spirit that inhabits the body of a willing host. It will eventually claim that form as its own. The host's body becomes misshapen under the weight of the evil energy—you saw how Charlie looked—but it's very strong." She read from the book: "From the time when man first took his place above the animals, the shamans understood man was capable of great evil that animals were not. This spirit, which embodied the evil in the hearts of men, was banished from the living plane."

"What language is that written in?" the sheriff asked.

"The whole book is in many languages because it came from different sources from all over the world. I only read German and French—and English, of course."

Sheriff Owens raised his eyebrows, looking impressed.

She gestured to a long column of handwritten notes alongside the foreign words, so neat they could have been typed. "Most of the rest has notes in English that summarize. This one is from a Welsh priest who says he translated it from a 'Norse farmer.'"

"Ho-ly hell." Sheriff Owens sat back hard, running his fingers through his hair. "So my official report will say that this was part of an occult ritual Charlie Logan had been planning for Mrs. Grant for some time. I'm not having something as crazy as the truth in my official record. I'll have a warrant put out for Charlie Logan—if that's even what he looks like now—and keep an eye on your family."

"What are we going to do *unofficially*?" Kevin asked. "I mean, if we find this thing, we can't just lock it up and give it a fair trial."

Sheriff Owens turned to Audrey. "What do you think we should do with him? Can we kill it or trap it or something?"

She scoured the page in her book then peered over at Charlie's book. "I could try to find the spell he used in his book and see if that says more." Her hand hovered just above the pages. "But my book says we'll have to kill it before it completely consumes the human host. After that..." She looked up at the sheriff. "Well, it just pretty much says there's no killing it after that."

Sheriff Owens screwed up his face into an indecipherable expression then gave a heavy sigh. He scratched at his head vigorously. "Christ, this is bad."

"No kidding," Ivy whispered.

The sheriff looked over at her, commiserating. "Sorry, kiddo."

"Then we find it before it completely takes over Charlie Logan. It looks like there's not much Charlie left right now," Kevin said. "How do we do that?"

"I don't know. We'll have to look into that, too, I guess." Audrey's shoulders slumped.

The sheriff slapped the table as if he'd come to a decision. "All right, then I guess all we can do is wait for you to look. I'll put out my warrant. I've got more than enough to arrest him if he's still recognizable. We know he injured Samuel Lovell and killed Liberty Walsh—and likely Arthur Bavery as well. We'll hope someone sees something unusual and calls it in." With a half-hearted shrug, he asked Audrey, "He would be doing something unusual, right?"

"I would imagine so," she answered. "I think 'unusual' would be a *best-case* scenario, though."

"He didn't seem to know how to be a person," Violet added. "And he's just overflowing with hatred. I would think he'd have to vent it before long."

"Let's just hope no one gets hurt," Sheriff Owens said to no one in particular. "Jesus, someone's gonna get hurt, aren't they?"

The group sat in silence for a few long seconds. Finally, Ivy's fears bubbled to the surface. "He'll come back for me. I know he will." She gathered several deep breaths. "He'll follow me wherever I am, especially now." Her eyes prickled with tears that she refused to shed.

Violet squeezed her shoulder reassuringly.

"No, it's fine." She squared her shoulders and took another deep breath. "I just mean that's how you'll find him. He'll come back here."

"We can put more protections on the house," Audrey said.

Charlie Logan was persistent, and the unnamed spirit that had claimed him certainly shared that determination. If they didn't fight back, he would eventually find a way to get to them.

"Even though this *thing* is taking over the man he used to be, why would he want Ivy? Why does the monster care about what Charlie wants?" Kevin asked. "That thing doesn't even know Ivy."

Violet answered, "In the basement, it said it wanted Charlie to have her, like, as a favor or something, for letting it out of wherever it was before. Or maybe it sort of takes on a little bit of the person it's inside of…"

"Charlie's its pet now." Ivy couldn't draw her eyes away from the book of dark magic. It sang to her, the same way it must have called to Charlie, telling her she needed its power. She almost wanted to let it consume her. Then she could let go of everything and just let it drown her—

Sheriff Owens cleared his throat, drawing her thoughts back to the people in the room with her and away from the flowing river of power. "I do think Ivy's right, though. I'll bet he comes back. He definitely has a long-term plan that involves her. He's too invested to give up now."

"We'll have someone watch the house," Kevin said without waiting for the sheriff's permission.

"I don't know what good that would do," Violet said gently. "You can't shoot it."

"What would you have me do?" he whispered rather harshly, directing the comment to Violet. His shoulders tensed with frustration that matched the desperation in his eyes.

"Bonniere, I think she means that they can handle it however they handle this stuff. I'll give you the reins to be here whenever you can."

Sheriff Owens stood, patting Kevin's shoulder. "Ladies, I guess I'll have to leave you to look things over, but you let me know right away if there's anything I can do or anything you need. I'll be in touch. Bonniere, I'll see you next shift."

He shook hands with Audrey and squeezed Ivy's arm lightly before leaving.

Chapter Twenty-Five

WHILE THE GIRLS TALKED WITH Kevin in the living room, Audrey gathered up her reading glasses, a notepad, and a pen. She scribbled notes about the spirit, copying from her own book: "Fire can kill it. Strongest at sunrise and sunset. Use white stone. Beware the new moon."

"He who calls it shall cast it out," she whispered, flipping to the following page. Another drawing depicted a crouching man swallowing a dark cloud. "Shoot!" she muttered, hoping that didn't mean she needed Charlie's participation to get rid of the spirit. He was too far gone to be reasoned with—that likely would have been impossible even before the spirit's influence over him strengthened, unless he'd realized his mistake. That thing would never serve him. It would only use him until it was strong enough to no longer need a human host.

"What does it want?" she asked herself, but she knew the answer. It had taken up Charlie Logan's interest in Ivy and had intensified its focus tenfold. It wanted nothing but evil, and Charlie had already given it purpose for that. Audrey only hoped she could figure out how to kill it before it could no longer be killed.

She placed a bookmark in her own book then closed it slowly, contemplating the other book. The thought of touching it still made her skin crawl. It practically stank of black magic. *And is that human skin?*

Her book was simply a collection of information, spells that could be used to call the powers of the moon, the sun, and the earth. Audrey's mother had taught her the magic that came from nature—it did not know evil or good. Knowing the differences and doing no harm was her responsibility. Nothing truly good ever came from using magic to harm another. A few

times, she'd thought the consequences might have been worth the effort...
But I missed that chance.

Convinced that she would have to touch the other book, she resolved to protect herself from its influence. Audrey went to the cabinet and pulled out a fat white candle. She struck a match and let it hover over the wick for a second. "Share with me your protection," she whispered to the spark while lighting the candle. For a moment, she watched the dancing flame and the melting wax that pooled around it. From the drawer at her hip, she carefully selected the oil. She plucked out her stone pestle and mortar then tapped a few drops of oil into the bowl and one drop in the palm of her hand. The scent of bergamot reminded her of Earl Grey tea. Holding the burning candle over the bowl, Audrey dripped wax into the oil then swished it with the pestle. Before it could harden, she dipped her fingertips in so that the pads were thick with a smooth layer of wax.

"That'll do, I suppose." She inspected the result.

Settling back down at the table, she pulled her notepad and pen closer but kept the book at arm's length. Uncertain where to start, she flipped a few pages and rolled her neck, trying to loosen the tension that had settled there. With a hard blink, Audrey steeled herself for the task.

The next hour was spent poring over the book, starting with the bookmarked pages. The markers were all hastily torn scraps of envelopes and newspaper. Charlie was the main suspect for the unceremonious treatment of the book. He clearly had felt its influence, but being the loser he was, he hadn't seen fit to treat even that power with respect. Most of the marked spells, old and new, were in English, and nearly all were meant to draw power or influence.

"No wonder..." She found the spell he'd managed to cast that had affected the entire town so that he could hide in plain sight after killing Libby Walsh. Then she found the spell he'd used to call the spirit. The drawing in his book was nearly identical to the one in hers. She skimmed the incantation but was afraid to read it in its entirety, even silently.

She took off her glasses and rubbed her eyes. Her notes filled entire pages of the steno pad next to her, but she felt as if she didn't know any more than she had when she started. The spirit inside Charlie Logan was ancient, almost as old as time. It was like the wildest, fiercest creature that had ever roamed the world. It was the darkness cast out of the hearts of men—evil given form.

That he'd managed to wreak so much havoc without anyone to lead him in magic was impressive. But Audrey hadn't received much training. Everything she'd learned had come from her mother and the family book. *Maybe Charlie Logan's family was magic.* He'd never given off an air of magic before, but magic always called to magic. Even if he hadn't possessed it when he was younger, it was only natural that he'd returned to Grant Farm after acquiring magic of his own.

A soft knock on the casement at the doorway drew Audrey from her contemplations.

"Mrs. Grant, do you have anything you would like me to relay to Sheriff Owens?" Kevin asked.

She rubbed her eyes again wearily, wishing she had a better answer for him—and herself. "No, Kevin, I don't believe I do." She sighed. His disappointed frown told her he'd been hoping for more. "But I will call him if I find something he can do or needs to know about."

"Well, I'll leave it at that, then. If any of you ladies need me, all you have to do is call." He wrote his number at the corner of the notepad and circled it.

"I'm sure you'll hear from one of us before long." She smiled despite herself.

A pale blush crept up from his collar. With a curt nod, he excused himself. Then Audrey heard Violet tell him goodbye.

Audrey sat staring at the tabletop, thoughts running through her head on an endless loop. Not one yielded useful results. *I'm missing something... I just have to be.* They would have to find Charlie Logan first.

A few minutes later, the doorbell chimed, then Violet stepped into the kitchen. "This is not a good time, but the guy from Good Stuffs is here for the fruit order for the store. Could you come out so we can go over what you guys agreed to?" She shrugged, spreading her hands in front of herself. "Sorry, I didn't know what to tell him, so I figured we might as well take care of it and get him out of here."

"All right." She took one last look at the book and her notes. Audrey grabbed the blue evidence bag and shook the book into it before she turned and followed Violet to the office.

Chapter Twenty-Six

IVY CANTED HER HEAD, STUDYING the notes lying on the table. Knowing that her grandmother's knowledge was incomplete, Ivy suspected that Audrey's research was incomplete as well. She pulled the tablet closer, deciphering Audrey's scribbles. Ivy glanced at the book, which was back in the bag. Her grandmother's book also lay on the table. It probably held much of the same information her own Book of Shadows did. Even if Audrey hadn't shown Ivy and Violet the source, she'd imparted much of her knowledge already. Audrey's magic was what Rhiannon called "old earth magic." Ivy had been surprised to find the same information in New Age books.

She looked over the oil and candle that Audrey had left sitting on the table. After repeating the process that she was sure her grandmother had carried out to protect herself from Charlie's malevolent book, Ivy slid it from the bag. Flipping through the marked pages, she saw that Audrey had already taken note of those. She skimmed hand-drawn diagrams of human anatomy, recipes that called for vile ingredients, and many pages written in languages that she could not read. She stopped on a page marked with a torn piece of paper—she recognized the blue lightning-bolt logo of the electric company. On the page marked by the scrap, a figure obscured by a smudge of soot hovered over a sleeping person. Ivy snarled at the drawing. *So he was the watcher.* Fueled by the knowledge that she hadn't imagined the darkness lurking in her dreams, she understood that she couldn't run from him. Ivy needed to put an end Charlie Logan.

She glanced at Audrey's notebook. *White stone? I would have guessed a black knife would contain the spirit.* "But then it would be concentrated, not dispersed. Maybe it's too strong when it's contained," she said aloud. If she needed white stone, she had just the thing.

She needed to call Rhiannon. Ivy grabbed her cell phone and saw that she'd missed a call from Morrison Realty, along with several from a number she didn't recognize. Mark was out of town, and Ivy wasn't in the mood for Karen's chipper conversation, so she decided to save that task for later. Instead, she dialed Rhiannon's number.

"Bewitching Word," Rhiannon chirped cheerfully. "How can I help you?" Rhiannon was the only real friend Ivy had made while at school—and the woman didn't even attend the university.

Ivy grinned, picturing her friend on the other end of the line. "Hello, Rhiannon."

"Ivy!" Rhiannon exclaimed. Then her voice turned serious. "What's wrong? Something happened."

"It did—and I need your help. Do you remember those dreams I was having?"

"Yes, with the strange presence." Ivy heard Rhiannon's fingernails tapping on the countertop. "Nightmares, more like it."

"Well, it's here. It's a man I used to know. He's done some kind of malevolent magic and conjured a spirit. He's already killed two people…" Her voice wavered into a high-pitched warble before she slowed her ramble. "Um, he's definitely after me, and he actually took me—"

"I knew it! I knew the cards weren't wrong. Why did you wait so long to call me?"

Ivy stifled a sob that came out of nowhere.

"Oh, Ivy, I'm sorry. What can I do?"

"I need some information. This thing—it's really bad. I should have called you sooner, but I just couldn't imagine that it would come to this. I still don't know how it got so close to home. I didn't think it would get me here." Tears tumbled from her eyes then slipped down her cheeks, unchecked. The emotion shouldn't have surprised her—lately, it seemed always just below the surface, ready to breach. "My gran seems stumped, too." She ran through Audrey's notes with Rhiannon, who stopped her to ask several questions at various points in the conversation. Ivy heard flipping pages and tarot cards being slapped down several times.

"So what do you think about the knife?" Ivy asked finally.

"Well, it doesn't actually say you need a white-handled knife. Maybe it does mean you need a white stone." Rhiannon sighed. "Stone magic just is not my forte, dear. I'm not sure I can be much help with that, but I suspect we're thinking the same thing."

After a heartbeat, they said in unison, "The opal knife."

Rhiannon clicked her tongue. "The gods knew you would need it when they brought it to you. It might be the very thing in the book."

Or my mother knew I would need it.

Rhiannon had many athames with stone handles, but she'd never seen one with a stone blade. When Ivy had first shown her the knife, Rhiannon had guessed it was probably worth a fortune, but Ivy couldn't bear to part with it. Anything that connected her to Rachel was precious.

"It might work, but it can't possibly be the exact tool in the spell, can it?" *Did my mother know Charlie Logan? She couldn't have...* Ivy suddenly had the sinking feeling that her mother might have been watching her all along. *But why would she hide from me?*

"Oh, strange things abound in this world, dear. Strange things..." Rhiannon sighed again. "But if you need a white stone, you already have one with great magic."

"Thanks, Rhiannon."

"Anytime, dear. Protect yourself, and call me again soon."

After hanging up the phone, Ivy went straight to her bedroom and knelt beside the bed then peered under it. She slid the pine box from its hiding place and opened it. The blade's whetted edge mesmerized her for a moment. "She must have known." A slow smile spread across her face.

Chapter Twenty-Seven

T HAT EVENING, IVY AND VIOLET stood at the edge of the porch with the bag of herbs and dust that Audrey had made. Each had a small wooden bowl.

"Let's start here"—Ivy waved toward the edge of the porch—"and we'll go around clockwise." She paused, thinking they should be taking the ritual more seriously. "Do you want to say something or…"

Violet shrugged. "Gran didn't say to, but we can if you want."

"In brightest day, in blackest night, let no evil escape my sight," Ivy chanted then scooped a handful from the bag and cast it in a wide arc across the yard.

"Was that the Green Lantern's oath?" Violet asked, her nose crinkled in amusement.

"This whole thing is beyond me, out of my realm, and I'm so scared that it's making me weird." Ivy's frustration had bled into her voice despite her attempt to sound calm.

"Yeah, we've never really done anything like this before," Violet said. "Never needed to." She was quiet for a second as Ivy dug her small wooden bowl into the powder in the bag.

"Do you think we're going to be all right?" Ivy searched Violet's face for an honest answer.

"Yeah, I think so." Violet nodded. "I mean, either Gran will figure this out, or something…" She smiled weakly. "Just knowing that it's there makes us more prepared."

Violet's voice echoed the dread weighing down Ivy's heart.

They continued sprinkling the powder around the house, finishing just as twilight fell. Ivy stole a glance through the kitchen window. Inside, Audrey was speaking into the phone while stirring a large pot on the stove.

"Violet?" Ivy asked quietly.

"Yeah?"

When Ivy didn't answer right away, Violet turned to look at her sister.

Ivy nervously twisted the pouch's drawstring around her fingers. "I know something that I should have told you and Gran before."

A shadow of concern fell over Violet's face. "What's wrong?"

"I met some people when I was in Chicago—this one woman in particular, who told me that I shimmered. It was really strange at first, but then she showed me some stuff and a book just like that one that Gran showed the sheriff."

Violet's eyes widened a little.

"My friend, Rhiannon, she did a tarot reading," Ivy said. "And, well, I'm afraid that I might have brought Charlie here. I think he's been in my dreams for a while."

Violet's face twisted in disgust. "That sounds awful, Ivy, but it's not your fault. He was here before you were. If anything, he brought *you* here."

"Maybe."

"Let's get back inside. It's getting dark."

When Violet and Ivy entered the house, Audrey was no longer stooped over the pot on the stove. She was sitting silently at the kitchen table, one elbow propped up on it, holding her hand against her forehead. Her other hand clutched the telephone. Ivy's eyes settled on the phone. A heavy wave of guilt pummeled her heart. She knew instantly who had called. Sam was dead, and it was her fault.

The next few days were a strange blur of police interviews and a procession of neighbors with casseroles. Karen Morrison had brought an armload of groceries and apologized profusely for Mark's absence because he was out of town.

Sam's funeral finally marked the passage of days filled with fear and grief. Ivy watched Beverly intently as the parade of mourners marched by her. The faraway look in her eyes made her seem lost, as if she were searching the crowd for someone she didn't really expect to see. She reminded Ivy of her grandmother at her grandfather's funeral. Audrey had been stoic, but she'd clung to anyone, even strangers, offering her comfort. Knowing she'd lost such a large piece of her heart, she seemed prepared to give the rest away to anyone who would take it. For all her ability, Audrey hadn't foreseen the heart attack that had taken their patriarch.

For a moment, Ivy imagined herself at Audrey's funeral, but she briskly shoved it aside before the emotion that went with it could overtake her. She suspected *she* would not be stoic. Ivy pulled her thoughts back to reality. A woman with a familiar face and a name that Ivy couldn't recall had just asked her a question. Ivy didn't remember the beginning of their conversation, and she wondered if she'd participated.

"I'm sorry. Could you say that again?" she said, doing her best to slip a polite tone into her voice.

"It's fine, dear." The woman patted Ivy's arm. "I was just asking if you think Beverly's going to be staying on the farm now that Sam's gone."

Ivy wished she could remember who the woman was so that she could decide if that was any of her business. "I'm pretty sure she's staying in our house for a while. She's welcome to stay indefinitely as far as we're concerned. We have room."

"My Jonathan might be looking for a place to stay, maybe help out on the farm."

Ivy suddenly put a name to the face when she recognized Jonathan's name. "Oh, Mrs. Taylor, you'll have to—"

"I'll talk to your grandmother about it, dear." And with that, Mrs. Taylor, always the good mother looking out for her sons—whom no one had ever accused of being industrious—had retrieved all the information she'd come for.

Ivy didn't relish the idea of Jonathan Taylor—or anyone, really—moving into Sam and Beverly's house. Jonathan would no doubt be little more than his mother's gossip hound. Ivy just hoped her grandmother felt the same. Audrey would no doubt agree that Mrs. Taylor had not chosen the proper time or place to bring up such a thing.

Mrs. Taylor's abrupt dismissal gave Ivy an opportunity to excuse herself from the crowd. She stood outside the country church, watching the silver-rimmed rainclouds skim the treetops. Though she hoped that meant good company was coming, Ivy knew better. She watched a woman load a red-haired little girl into a sedan. Like so many people in town, the woman looked familiar, but Ivy didn't seem able to put a name to her face. A sudden pang of guilt—or remorse maybe—struck her as she wondered if there was any place in the world where she knew the people who surrounded her. *It's probably my fault that I keep too much to myself.*

She turned away from the flow of people leaving the church, heading for their cars, and followed a little stone path through overgrown hedges around the back of the church. Beverly and Audrey were sitting on a wooden bench, their backs to her. Ivy almost spoke, then she heard their conversation and drew back into the bushes, not wanting to interrupt.

"I don't know how you do it," Beverly said. "Not having Jack and not knowing about Rachel…" She closed her eyes. A lone, silent tear streaked down her face. "I just miss my Sam so much, and it's only been a few days. At least I know he's okay now. With Rachel…"

"There's really nothing to explain how you feel when your child's gone." Audrey lowered her eyes to her clasped hands in her lap. "Even when you think it's probably her own decision, you still wonder where she is and if she's hurt, if she's happy… if she's still alive." A heavy silence stifled the conversation for a second as the two women stared ahead, out at the trees separating the fields from the churchyard where Beverly had just buried her husband.

Ivy swallowed air, trying to breathe quietly, even though she felt as if she were sucking in all the air for miles around.

"The truth is, I don't know where she is, and I don't think she wants to be found either way. Jack and I decided a long time ago that we were just going to let her make her own decisions. There's no turning back time, so we just have to live with the way we raised her. We had two more girls to take care of when she left, and we focused on doing that better." She looked over at her friend. "And when I lost Jack… well, I think everyone does that differently. Losing their sweetheart, I mean." She patted Beverly's hand. "And the girls and I will always keep you around if you'll have us."

"Oh, Aud, I think you're probably stuck with me." Beverly put an arm around Audrey's shoulders and gave her a squeeze.

Not wanting to be caught eavesdropping, Ivy tiptoed back around the path and slipped back into the church kitchen, where she found Violet cleaning up. Watching her sister for a moment, Ivy wondered, as she often did, if Violet looked like their mother and if she herself might look like their father. *Whoever that is…* She shook off the thought, knowing that train never took her anywhere good, and went to help her sister.

Chapter Twenty-Eight

A LONG, LONESOME HOWL BROKE THE silence that shrouded the farmhouse as the women sat around the table, a cup of tea before each of them. The sound stole the breath from Audrey's throat. Charged air danced across her arms, and her fingers squeezed the teacup. Her knuckles had turned white, stark against the black china that had been a wedding gift from her mother.

For days, an oppressive blanket of expectation had covered the house and the lives of the women in it. Even as they settled into an uneasy routine, the anticipation of impending catastrophe lurked in every action, every thought of the next moment.

"Damn coyotes!" Beverly murmured then returned to her solemn task of signing the thank-you notes intended for the people who had attended Sam's funeral. After scribbling her name, she passed a note to Ivy, who slipped it into an envelope and sealed it.

"This is a lot of notes, Bev." Violet slapped a stamp onto the envelope.

"Well, Sam knew a lot of people—"

An unseen visitor rapped at the door. It was a simple, heavy knock—not the knock of someone friendly. Frozen, the women looked around the table at each other. Bev's eyes were closed tightly as if she might render herself invisible that way. No one moved to answer the door.

The cats stalking the yard under the cover of darkness suddenly gathered their voices together in a horrible yowling refrain that matched the wail of the wind. The piercing caterwaul rose to an overwhelming volume before a scuffling sound cut it short. A few long seconds later, another knock made them all start in their seats. The sound of a fist meeting wood seemed to materialize from every direction, every wall, at once. The broom propped against the door tottered and clattered to the floor.

"It's him!" Ivy whispered. The color drained from her face, but her cheeks were flushed.

"Would he just knock like that?" Violet whispered to her grandmother.

"Maybe he has to." Audrey shrugged, slightly bewildered, her stomach clenched in knots. She had foolishly dared to hope that Charlie would simply leave her granddaughter alone once he realized the house was protected. "I've been putting protection on this house and you girls for years. Maybe he just can't get past." Her calm demeanor belied a fierce fear inside her.

As if unwilling to wait for another warning, Violet crept to the window and peered through the slit in the curtains beside the front door, careful not to disturb the cloth. "There's nobody out there," she hissed.

Beverly and Audrey scrambled away from the table to look outside from different vantage points. Audrey had expected to see something sinister waiting just outside. Only a pale pool of white moonlight threw faint shadows across the rickety porch.

Drawing short, sharp breaths, Ivy hesitated just inside the doorway between the kitchen and the living room. Her grip on the back of the reclining chair was so tight that her fingers seemed to sink into the dark-green cloth.

Another insistent whack rattled through the sturdy house. Strings on the upright Wurlitzer in the hall reverberated, the first time the piano had made a sound in months. Violet recoiled from the window with a gasp then crouched below the windowsill. She disappeared from view behind the sofa.

"Nobody in the back," Bev's disembodied voice called quietly from the back door.

Static electricity crawled across Audrey's skin as anxiety rushed through her veins. She stood tensely in the middle of the space, uncertain where to turn. Flicking the switch, she killed the lights that made them visible to whatever lay beyond the inky glass of the windowpanes.

As her eyes slowly adjusted to the darkness, several silent heartbeats followed, and the women waited for another sound. Audrey's shoulders relaxed a little with each second that passed. But fear of the unknown smothered her with its quietude.

Violet stood up and shrugged. "Is it gone?"

As if in answer, a succession of louder thumping cascaded against the house. Ivy let out a small squeak and sank to the floor behind the chair, in tears. Her arms curled around her head to hide the sobs that wracked her frame. Audrey knelt next to her and wrapped her arms around Ivy. Violet was riveted to the floor where she stood. The air crackled with tiny sparks of electricity as Violet struggled to control her anger and frustration. Audrey almost hoped the girl's emotions *would* boil over.

"He's everywhere, and he's going to get me sooner or later," Ivy cried with wild fear that had broken loose inside her. The noise that continued to rattle the house stopped abruptly, and an incorporeal voice answered her cry.

"Ivy… come to me…" the lilting voice called out to her sweetly from the darkness.

"No!" she shouted with wide, terror-stricken eyes. Her face was wet with tears that she made no attempt to wipe away.

"Come to me!" the voice demanded with a shriek that blew open the exterior doors. The screen doors smacked against the house's siding. A blast of cold air streaked through the room.

In the kitchen, a chair clattered to the floor, and Bev yelped. The gust of air whipped papers and envelopes from the roll-top desk in the dining room and sent them sailing through the air. In the living room, curtains caught by the wind slapped against Violet's face and arms and tangled around her.

"It's okay. He can't get inside," Audrey said as she huddled on the floor with Ivy, clinging to her tightly. Then the air, as if it had taken physical form, tugged at Ivy and threatened to rip her from Audrey's grip. Ivy's arms were slick with cold sweat, and Audrey could feel her granddaughter slipping from her grasp.

"Oh, no," Ivy whispered in horror as the ghoulish air pulled her loose, and she slid across the floorboards toward the door. Sprawled on her stomach, Ivy stretched, reaching out for Audrey. Ivy's fingernails scrabbled against the wooden floor.

Audrey jumped up just as Violet pulled the entire window treatment from the wall, ending her struggle with the curtains. The clattering release propelled Violet forward until she was on top of Ivy, enveloping her in the cloth and stopping her slide.

Audrey pushed against the wind and stomped past the girls tangled together beneath the curtains on the floor. She gripped the doorframe and thrust herself beyond the opening, looking for an entity to unleash her anger upon.

"You don't get to have her!" she bellowed over the roar of the rushing air. She raced off the porch and into the grass, expecting to be met with violence. But beyond the perimeter of the door, the thick air was calm. An approaching pack of coyotes howled in an eerie, rising chorus as they raced through the cornfield.

Several tense barn cats waited atop the clothesline poles. Eyes wide and frightened, they looked desperate to be under better cover but afraid to light on solid ground. Their cumulative stare shifted, and she followed its path. A shady apparition flitted between the barn and a smaller shed, making its way to Beverly and Sam's house, hiding behind trees and bushes as it went.

"What...?" Audrey whispered. She had simply expected something bolder from Charlie Logan. Two coyotes burst from the cornstalks, followed by several more. Audrey shrank back against the house. As they yipped and howled, they targeted something behind the other house. Their excited sounds told her they had found what they were looking for. Her boldness had faded, and she retreated inside, where the wind no longer blew. In the kitchen, Beverly had closed the back door and was leaning against it, watching intently through the window.

Violet sat on the floor, hugging Ivy. She smoothed her sister's hair as Ivy sobbed silently into her hands. "What's outside?"

Audrey shook her head. She wasn't certain if Charlie had sent the thing outside in his stead or if he'd come himself. If the spirit had come, she knew that coyotes wouldn't have been much of a match for it. "I don't know, but I think the coyotes might have gotten it."

Chapter Twenty-Nine

I VY WOKE LATE IN THE afternoon after a restless night huddled together with the other women in front of the fireplace. Despite being grown women, none of them had relished the idea of sleeping, or being alone, in the dark. After an early lunch, they had settled in the living room, where Ivy had fallen asleep.

She stayed snuggled on the couch with her grandmother while Bev snored in the armchair, a bag of melted ice wilted over her propped-up ankle. Bev was lucky she'd only twisted when flipping over her kitchen chair. Violet peeked around the corner from the kitchen and gave a little wave when she saw Ivy was awake. Ivy smiled back, but she wasn't ready to leave the protective cocoon of her grandmother's embrace, beneath the quilt they had sewn together when she was a child just learning to sew. When Violet disappeared back into the kitchen, Ivy traced the edges of the fabric squares. Some of the lines were crooked, but she remembered how proud she'd been of each stitch.

"Awake, are we?" Audrey whispered.

"Violet's up," Ivy answered quietly.

Bev shifted but didn't open her eyes. "She's been up for hours, doing God knows what. I don't know if she slept at all." Ivy hadn't heard Bev stop snoring. "It's almost dinnertime."

Violet's phone played a little tune, then a metallic clang propelled the three women in the living room from their pretend sleep. Beverly kicked forward in the chair. Her leg fell off the rest, and she winced. But Ivy was the first to spring into standing position.

"What?" Violet was still out of sight, but the metal bowl she'd dropped circled in a wide arc along the hardwood.

Ivy rounded the edge of the tall pantry cabinet, followed closely by her grandmother and a limping Bev, to find Violet with her cell phone pressed tightly to her ear. She was staring at the floor, gesturing with her hands.

"No. I don't…" Violet looked up at the women and seemed to suddenly realize they were standing there. "I don't think we should." Her shoulders slumped a little—Violet had just given an answer she knew was not the right one. "Fine," she said quietly, turning away. "You'll be here in, like, five minutes, then?" She nodded. "All right." She flipped the phone shut and locked eyes with Audrey. "He took a little girl."

Ivy's heart sank.

"Kevin said she looked like Ivy." Violet didn't meet her sister's eyes, looking instead at her grandmother.

A deep pit opened up in Ivy's core, and she knew she would have to fill it with courage rather than fear, because she would have to be the one to end this—to end Charlie Logan and the thing he had become.

Violet paced awkwardly, waiting for the timer on the oven. Still, she started when it buzzed. She took out the apple pie, which she knew no one would eat, and set it on the stovetop. When the doorbell rang, she was staring absentmindedly at the pie. She heard her grandmother answer the door, then everyone, including Kevin and Sheriff Owens, gathered in the kitchen. Though Violet hadn't mentioned their ominous visitor the night before, Kevin looked at her intently, concern etched on his face. *I must look like hell.* The other women looked tired and rumpled, and they had slept longer than she had.

Without making any attempt at greeting or small talk, Sheriff Owens launched into the important part. "So we got a report of an intruder, and the parents—actually, just the mom—didn't see him come up to the house, only heard a snuffling like a dog or something. It was broad daylight, and the girl was right inside the back door or maybe on the porch. Her mother was in the next room. She heard the girl call out, and she found the back door wide open. She went outside to see what she described as a tall, broad-shouldered man jump the fence like it was nothing—it's a five-foot chain-link—and run across the road into the woods. 'Like an animal,' she said.

She couldn't find her daughter, thought he might have been carrying her, and she called the police immediately."

"And you think this is Charlie Logan?" Bev asked, raising an eyebrow. She hadn't seen how much Charlie had changed. Her skepticism was understandable.

"The last time I saw him, he moved like an animal," Violet offered. "On all fours."

Sheriff Owens pulled a wallet-sized photo from the breast pocket of his uniform. "This is why we think it's Charlie Logan." He held the photo out to Audrey.

Though Ivy made no effort to look at the photograph, Violet peered over her grandmother's shoulder as she and Beverly murmured their understanding. The girl in the picture was a dead ringer for Ivy when she was around age ten, right down to the chestnut-brown braid.

"He took her in broad daylight?" Audrey asked. "Even as noticeable as he is now?"

"He'll be strongest during the new moon, tomorrow night. It doesn't matter if he gets noticed anymore," Ivy said. "He's strongest at sundown and sunrise, and he's planning something."

"Let's hope it's for sunrise," Kevin said, looking out the window. He checked his watch. "Sunset is in about an hour."

"Do you have any idea where he might have taken a little girl?" Sheriff Owens asked. "Do you think you could help us find him?"

"I don't think we should get any more involved than we already are," Violet said quietly. The sheriff's question had been directed toward her grandmother, but Violet knew what Audrey's answer would have been. She almost didn't want Kevin to hear, even though she'd said it to him once already—or maybe *because* she'd said it once already. "We're not police officers, I mean. Aren't people going to wonder why we keep hanging around?" She'd looked through her grandmother's book as well as Charlie's. She was certain nothing in either would lead them to his lair.

"No one else understands what's going on here," Kevin answered, drawing her into a private conversation as the others continued talking among themselves.

I've apparently been outvoted anyway.

Kevin touched her arm tentatively, as if expecting a static shock, then pulled her aside just a little. Realizing she hadn't been much of an influence on her grandmother's decision, she let him lead her away.

"Look, regardless of what other people think is going on, the people in your family are the only ones who could stop him. Even if the police department finds him, they won't have any idea what to do with him."

"And now it's about more than just us," she finished for him. He wouldn't go so far as to call her selfish for putting her fears ahead of a little girl's safety, but she could tell he wanted to say it.

"Yeah," he whispered.

Still uncertain, Violet only nodded.

"You'll be like consultants, if that makes you feel better. You know the suspect, and that makes your opinion valuable, regardless of any of the other stuff you and I know went on." The sheriff addressed everyone in the room, but Violet realized his words were meant for her. "Gillian Fuller—that's the little girl—her mother's not going to care who you are, not if you can help."

"Violet, we can at least go look at the house and see what's there," Audrey said gently. "We can't not help that little girl, Vi."

She nodded again. "Then we don't have time to stand around talking, or we'll be out there in the dark."

Bev shuffled to a chair and sat down. "I'll be staying here, then. My leg's not up for traipsing around in the woods after last night."

Kevin cut his gaze sharply toward Violet, a questioning look on his face. She waved him off without explaining how Beverly had hurt herself, thinking he would overreact. For half a heartbeat, she wondered if she might prefer him to overreact and tell them not to come. But her grandmother was right—they had to do something.

"I'll be right back," Ivy said then raced up the stairs toward her room.

When the others turned away to talk around the table, Kevin took Violet's hand and pulled her back. "What happened last night? You started to say something on the phone."

"I think he was here but couldn't get inside. Apparently, he found something else to keep him busy." Violet cringed at her sarcasm, which had sounded painfully harsh.

Kevin sighed then opened his mouth to speak, but Ivy interrupted him. "Let's go," she announced as if she'd suddenly become the one in charge.

Ivy slung a purse over her shoulder and marched toward the door. Violet noticed she'd changed her shirt. She glanced down at her clothes and deemed her jeans and dark-blue camp shirt appropriate for the task at hand. Ivy climbed into the front passenger seat of Kevin's car, and Violet slid into the backseat with Audrey. She half expected some kind of planning to happen during the ride, but they rode mostly in silence as Kevin followed Sheriff Owens to the Fuller house.

"Where's the little girl's father?" Violet asked. "I can't place the name."

"Afghanistan, I believe," Kevin answered. "I think Sheriff said he's due back in a month or two."

"Oh, hell," Violet said. That added a little more weight to the guilt she would have to carry if they couldn't bring Mrs. Fuller's daughter back to her.

The house wasn't really what Violet had anticipated. The unassuming yellow ranch seemed far too simple for a place where something as awful as a kidnapping had taken place. She wondered if Charlie had been watching the little girl since he'd lost Ivy. Perhaps that was how he'd kept busy while they'd been going about their lives, burying Sam in the process.

An unmarked police car was sitting in the drive. And Jeff Reynolds was standing on the porch, talking with a young woman who could have been Ivy's sister, though she looked nothing like Violet. If Charlie Logan had wanted a grown substitute for Ivy, Gillian's mother would have sufficed. He obviously missed the child version, though. The thought swelled into terror, which she tampered down with the reassurance that they would find the girl in time. He probably wouldn't really touch the girl and was holding onto Ivy as his main target. Gillian Fuller was just bait. Whether the human or the creature was making the decisions, Charlie was sharp enough to recognize that a child gave him more emotional leverage than an adult would have. All Violet's uncertainty about helping find the girl washed away, and she didn't care if Detective Reynolds knew that they had come to use witchcraft to solve his case.

Chapter Thirty

As soon as she stepped out of the car, Ivy felt the lingering trail of Charlie's magic. She experienced everything in slow motion: the breeze blowing through the grass where Charlie had stood, sun glinting off the chain-link fence where he had touched it, and the disturbed branches where he had stepped into the forest. He'd left the trail just for her. She could smell him in the air. The acrid wake of rippling atmosphere oozed over her, choking her and filling her stomach. He smelled of burnt hair and black magic. The vibration nearly tugged her toward the woods, but she forced herself to focus on Sheriff Owens.

"You feel that?" Violet whispered as they followed the sheriff to the house.

"Feel what?" Kevin asked.

Ivy nodded. "He's definitely been here." The knife, which she'd retrieved from her room just before leaving the house, pressed against the small of her back. She itched to hold it in her hand, to give herself that extra comfort.

On the porch, the sheriff quickly explained to Detective Reynolds that he'd brought the women just to look around, maybe offer moral support to the Fullers since they'd had their own brush with Charlie Logan. The detective didn't stick around, saying he was on his way back to his desk to issue an AMBER alert and organize a search party before dark. Sheriff Owens glanced discreetly at Audrey before nodding his approval. Mrs. Fuller stood patiently, wringing her hands, during the exchange. Ivy noted that Gillian had inherited her hair color from her mother.

Sheriff Owens introduced the Grants. "They're here sort of as a preliminary search party. Our suspect worked on their farm, and they recently had their own encounter with him."

"Whatever you need from me, just ask," Mrs. Fuller said, giving them each an imploring look. "I just need my Gillian back." Without waiting for instruction, she turned and gestured for them to follow. "I'll show you where we were."

As she followed Mrs. Fuller into the house, Ivy noted that her grandmother was silently looking around as if she were trying to memorize every detail. The front door opened into a large kitchen, and another door just around the corner went straight to the backyard. The smallish house seemed empty and open compared to the Grants' big, cluttered farmhouse.

"I was here." Mrs. Fuller pointed toward the sink by the window overlooking the yard. Then she led them to a porch on the back of the house, her calm, matter-of-fact demeanor representative of a soldier's wife.

In the backyard, another uniformed officer was taking photos with a digital camera. Behind him, the sun was suddenly sinking faster than Ivy wanted it to.

Mrs. Fuller pointed to a plastic playhouse on the porch. "I think she was inside, but Gillian had been playing here earlier. Maybe she came out to get something she'd left in the playhouse." She swung her arm toward the fence. "And he went over the fence there."

The officer by the swing set raised his hand in greeting but did not smile. Sheriff Owens nodded back, equally solemn.

Mrs. Fuller turned to Sheriff Owens, her eyes downcast. "She's in her nightgown. Dinner was a mess, so she took a bath early. I was worried about cleaning up… I should have been watching her." She swallowed hard but did not let her tears fall.

The sheriff put a hand on her shoulder. "This is not your fault. You were not being neglectful by letting your daughter play alone ten feet from you."

She gave him a sharp nod.

"We'll go ahead and start over that way, by the fence, and see what we can find. You stay here in case there's any news, all right?"

"Okay." She stood on the porch, hugging herself, as Violet and the others walked away. No one said anything else to Mrs. Fuller, and Ivy felt as though she should have, but she couldn't find the words.

"Well, this is the place," Sheriff Owens said, opening the gate in the chain-link fence and ushering them through it. "Does anything seem unusual?"

"Yeah," Ivy whispered, barely able to restrain herself.

The sheriff looked in the direction she was staring, past the street and into the woods. "Yeah?"

Violet nodded. "There's something here. He left it for us."

"Let's go, then," Sheriff Owens said, checking up and down the road before crossing.

Feeling like a hound set loose on a trail, Ivy rushed along the path through the woods.

"Slow down, Ivy," Audrey said. "Dusk is falling. We don't want to get separated at sunset."

"Sorry. It's just like it's… pulling me." She couldn't drag her eyes away from every little disturbed branch and leaf on the ground. Each bent blade of grass seemed to shout at her that Charlie had been through there.

Ivy… The wind seemed to whisper her name, and she froze, straining to listen for the source, willing it to speak again.

"What the hell was that?" Kevin asked, his hand on his gun. "Did you hear that?"

Ivy! The word came from nowhere and everywhere at once.

"It's him," Violet whispered.

Audrey took Ivy's arm. "You stay close here."

Ivy's body was rigid with tension. She felt his spell reeling her in, and she vaguely recognized the sensation from the night the silver mist had danced in the air. Audrey tugged gently on her arm, and Ivy forced herself to a stop. Glittery sparks twinkled around them. They were not lightning bugs, as she'd thought they were—his magic flittered in the air around her. *Not good.*

A haunting animal howl split the air, curdling Ivy's blood. She spun, thinking she'd heard something move off to her right.

Kevin and the sheriff both drew their guns and held them at the ready, pointed to the ground. Violet moved closer to Ivy.

From Ivy's left, another howl answered the first. She spun back around, nearly knocking Violet to the ground. Charlie was calling her, and something deep down in her lizard brain yearned to answer. An overwhelming urge rushed through her—to return the call with her own howl of anger, to tell him that she would be the one to finish his game. She was the foxhound, not the fox.

She couldn't stand the feeling of panic that enveloped her a moment longer. Violet grabbed the back of her shirt, but Ivy broke away from her, sprinting with her arms raised to keep low-hanging branches from whipping her face. Ivy couldn't see, but she knew she was moving closer to him. She followed his magic blindly as if she were pulling herself hand over hand along a rope in the darkness.

"Ivy, wait! He's teasing you," Audrey called as she thrashed through the brush. "Dammit, Ivy! Don't listen to him!"

As the others crashed through the woods behind her, Ivy pumped her legs harder, trying to reach the voice. A taunting cackle from the darkness propelled her forward across a bumpy field. She hadn't even realized she'd left the woods. But without the trees to obscure the view, she saw that the sky was dark. Still, the stars seemed bright without the moon there to steal the glare.

Her need to be free from the web of evil that Charlie Logan had been spinning around her overwhelmed her common sense and cautious nature. As she ran, the need to end the dance combined with the need to dance with Charlie Logan, to be near him, to be with him.

"Stop!" Violet shouted from behind her. "You don't know where you're going!" She was faster than the others and followed closely behind Ivy, making angry huffing sounds.

At almost the same instant, Ivy's foot slipped on slick ground. Her arms flapped uselessly as she desperately tried to stop both her fall and her forward momentum at the same time. But instead of landing flat on her back, she slid down the small incline just beyond the slick clay earth. The timber and empty, grassy fields gave way to small, deep lakes and ponds left behind when the strip mines were abandoned decades before. In the darkness, they were practically invisible to anyone rushing headlong into them.

She slid off the shallow ledge, and her body felt weightless for a short second before she fell. She writhed blindly. Unsure how far she would fall or how far away the ground was, she grasped at the empty air around her, trying in vain to touch something. She smacked the water with a ringing splash then sank below the surface.

When she rose, she gasped, trying to replace the air that had been forced from her lungs during her impact with the water. Disoriented, she thrashed around, trying to regain her bearings.

"Ivy?" Violet called out cautiously from the edge of the lake.

"Yes," Ivy called back. "I fell in the lake." She treaded water slowly, still trying to discern direction in the darkness.

"No kidding," Violet responded dryly. "Come this way, and I'll pull you out."

Listening carefully to her sister's voice echoing off the water, Ivy dog-paddled toward the sound. Violet hummed a short tune, and something plunked into the water, sending a glowing ripple of blue light across the lake's surface. Ivy followed the light to the water's edge, where Violet's form slowly came into focus. She was kneeling in the grass, leaning down over the ledge that dropped into the lake. Violet's outstretched hand was just above Ivy's head. Planting her feet into the mud, Ivy grasped her sister's forearm, and Violet did the same. Violet pulled as Ivy pushed against the muddy ledge and hefted herself flat onto her stomach in the grass.

"Why is the water so low?" Ivy got to her feet. She was dripping wet, unsure what was water and what was mud.

"It's just been dry for a couple of summers." Violet shook the water from her arm. "The rain a few days ago made the banks wet but didn't really fill in the lake."

An approaching rustle in the grass nearby warned that they were not alone in the clearing. They each tensed. Charlie must have doubled back on her after she'd fallen in the lake. Her dip into the cool water had apparently broken the spell over her because she no longer wanted to be anywhere near him.

Afraid she had become the hunted fox, she held her breath as she strained to listen for more movement. But instead of an attacking blow, a beam of light fell across her face. A hand shielded the sisters from the flashlight's full luminosity, but the light was still bright enough to prevent Ivy from identifying the shadowed person who held it.

"Are you fucking kidding me running off in the dark like that?" Kevin Bonniere's hushed voice hissed from the darkness beyond the light. He sounded angrier than she'd imagined the shy man could be. "This thing is *dangerous*, and Sheriff and I are carrying firearms. I could have *shot* you."

"Sorry," Violet spat back as Kevin lifted the flashlight's beam to her face. "We don't chase fleeing offenders for our day jobs, Kevin. *You* wanted us to help. I didn't tell you to get that gun out."

She lurched forward and pushed his arm away. "Get that out of my face. We won't be able to see in the dark if you blind us."

The light clicked off, and Kevin let out a quiet string of what sounded like French curse words—the first time she'd heard more than a little of his accent slip through.

"I just don't want to be out here, looking for *you*, when we're trying to find this little girl," he answered quietly. His anger had fizzled. "Just be careful, for chrissakes."

"Sorry," Ivy answered meekly, uncertain if he'd been talking to her or Violet—or both. "I just—"

"It's the magic," Violet interrupted. "It's hard, I know. But you've got to keep it together." She heaved a sigh. "I am not going to let him take you again." Ignoring Ivy's soaking clothes, Violet grabbed her and hugged her tightly.

Despite the broken connection, Ivy could still feel Charlie's presence all around her. His animal musk floated in the air, riding his magic like a wave. She had known the spirit creature was strong, but she hadn't realized how deep he'd managed to burrow under her skin.

Sheriff Owens and Audrey, who was puffing quite a bit, came up next to them. Gran leaned forward, her hands on her knees, catching her breath.

"Are we all in one piece?" she asked.

"Yeah," Ivy answered.

Audrey straightened and grabbed for Ivy. She pulled her granddaughter to her and whispered, "No more of that! Stay grounded when you feel like that. You need to be touching me or Violet if you think you can't feel yourself anymore. Remember what you know."

"Sorry, Gran."

"What are we doing now? Where do we go?" Sheriff Owens asked, looking around nervously. "We stick together, for sure. He's trying to separate you from the group—that much is obvious." He pointed at Ivy, his gestures odd outlines in the darkness, where disembodied voices hovered.

Ivy pulled several sheets of paper and a matchbook from the pocket of her jeans. They were soggy, ruined, but she remembered the words she'd written there before. "I can call the spirit, Gran. I think I have a spell that will work."

Silence answered her, so she explained. "I talked to my friend—she practices Wicca. Anyway, we think we know what the white stone is, and I wrote my own calling spell." She touched the knife clipped onto her belt at the small of her back.

"The one who calls it can kill it," Audrey answered. Ivy thought she was nodding in the darkness.

"Well, folks, I think we've got a problem. What are we going to do when we get it?" Kevin raised his arms then let his hands fall to his sides. "We're after the girl, not him. I don't know if getting him here is going to do any good if you're going to kill him. We need to get to where he has the girl."

If she's dead, we'll never find her. Ivy didn't voice the thought that she was sure the sheriff was thinking.

"She might be confined somewhere, running out of air, and if that's the case, then we can't just kill him and hope the search team finds her. And we have no leads to follow about this thing that's making the decisions here." Sheriff Owens's words dashed Ivy's last little glimmer of hope.

"Could we lure him here then follow him back to the girl?" Kevin asked. "Do you think he would be dumb enough to go straight back?" He directed the question at Audrey as if she were the expert on evil spirits. She was probably as close as they would get to that just then.

Audrey shrugged and turned to Ivy. "Can you follow him like you did before, when we were at the house?"

The oppressive pull was gone, along with the trail that she'd followed into the forest. Everything around her seemed dull and empty of Charlie Logan's dark magic. In that second, she imagined that it had all been a dream. The certainty of doom seemed foolish, and she felt useless, standing in the open darkness while her sister and grandmother stared at her, and the county sheriff and police officer looked on. She shook her head. "The connection's gone."

"What are our options, then?" Kevin asked no one in particular. "We don't have any real clues to follow because this guy is not the typical suspect." He looked up at Violet then at Ivy before turning to Sheriff Owens. "I don't know how else we're going to find that girl. I shot that thing once already, and it only laughed at me. When it touched me, I had this feeling, Sheriff. It wasn't like anything I know of. It was like this anger and just plain meanness sank into me." He rubbed the back of his neck nervously. "I've never been that scared before. Like being underwater and feeling like it would be a relief to just breathe in the water. I think even if we don't know where the girl is, if he's here, then we'll know he's not with her. So get him here, whatever it takes. Even if she's confined, she's better off without him there."

"Do it," Violet said quietly to Ivy as if the sheriff's opinion were moot. "What do you need?"

"Something to write with." Ivy squatted and felt the ground for a stick or sharp rock and came up empty. Her original spell involved using the matches to set the paper alight, but that was no longer an option. "Could you turn on the light for a second, Kevin?"

The light clicked on, his fingers covering it again, and Ivy spotted a patch of sandy soil nearby. Using her finger, Ivy drew a circle then scratched Charlie Logan's name in the dirt inside the circle. Improvising, she placed her palm over his name and recited the words of the spell, imagining his face. She had no idea how soon—or if—it would work. Right away, magic tugged at the pit of her stomach as if a cord had been wrapped around her torso and extended the length of her arm pressed to the ground. When she stood, that magic coursed away from her as if she'd thrown a net of it over the forest and kept hold of the strings. She stumbled forward a few steps, jerked off balance by the force of the net as it continued forward. Then it pulled taut, having found its mark. The net condensed to a tight lasso looped around Charlie Logan, she suspected—and hoped. He wasn't far. That hope urged her forward toward the trees, and she followed cautiously, the others right on her heels.

"What's happening?" Sheriff Owens asked from behind her.

Ivy—focused on the cord, trying not to slip and fall into a trap—did not answer.

"I think we're going to him," Violet said.

Several yards ahead, a void in the darkness slipped between trees at the edge of the clearing, stopping Ivy. Violet and the others recoiled then stood their ground around Ivy. The figure moved closer, drawn by Ivy's magic. She concentrated on pulling him closer, but when the darkness revealed the shape of Charlie Logan's misshapen form, her concentration wavered. She panicked and let the cord of magic slip from her fingers. Like a craven wolf set loose from a leash, the beast roared, eyes aflame once again, and charged them. Then suddenly, the spirit seemed to regain composure and recall its intention. She grasped for the magic cord, but it was gone. Licking her lips, she prepared to repeat the incantation.

"Come with me, Ivy," the voice rumbled, silken and appealing. "I'll set you free."

"You come to *me*!" she shouted back, feigning confidence while resisting the urge to reach for the knife case snapped to the belt loop at the back of her jeans. Briefly, she wondered what he meant by setting her free. *What does he think has trapped me?*

Something touched her arm, making her jump. She'd forgotten for a second that the others were there. Her grandmother held fast to her forearm, giving her strength. "Say it again."

"Oh, Audrey, let me have your lost little lamb," Charlie cooed, making Ivy's skin crawl. He moved and was nearly on them in a flash, only yards away.

"Holy shit!" Kevin said under his breath.

Then Charlie jerked forward and snapped his teeth at Ivy before turning and melting into the shadows.

"Go!" Sheriff Owens shouted.

They crashed through the brush and trees, but their quarry moved deftly and quickly through the darkness. And he was soon gone from their sight.

"Dammit!" Sheriff Owens howled into the darkness. "This is ridiculous! How are we supposed to find this thing?" He whirled to glare at Audrey, a fire in his eyes.

Kevin stepped between them, his hands spread at his sides. "Look, he must have a hideout or something near here. Why else would he come out here? What's out this way—a hunter's cabin or something?"

"There might be something like that," Audrey said quietly, "but we really aren't dealing with a person anymore. He might not be having rational thoughts. Now he's like a wild animal, just serving itself."

The sheriff eyed the woods warily. "You think he's lured us out here just to toy with us?"

"Not you, not Kevin." Violet shook her head. "Us," she said, gesturing to herself and Audrey.

"He came here for *me*," Ivy said quietly.

"That doesn't make them safe or anything." Violet pointed to the men.

Ivy shook her head. "He wants you, and them, to go away. He's not trying to lose me. He's trying to lose *you*. I'm obviously supposed to follow." Her voice quavered with fear despite her attempts to sound adamant. She would have to face him alone sooner or later.

"We need to find him… or it… first." Kevin swallowed hard, his gaze lingering on Violet.

"We"—Sheriff Owens jerked his thumb back and forth between himself and Kevin—"are responsible for that little girl." He drew his hands to his hips. "That's all there is to it."

"We'll find him." Audrey looked around the small clearing where they stood. "I need a coin."

The men looked puzzled, but Violet dug into her pockets without hesitation. The others followed suit. Only the sheriff produced anything useful. He pulled two quarters from his pants pocket and dropped them into Audrey's open palm.

"Perfect." She turned to a nearby maple tree, its trunk bigger than the rest. "We need to know where he went. He stole a child, and he is very dangerous. Please tell us where he went," she whispered to it sweetly as she patted its bark affectionately.

Violet handed her grandmother a broken stick, which Audrey used to dig a small hole at the base of the tree. Once the coins were nestled in the hole, she spread loose dirt and leaves over it.

She gestured for the girls to move closer. Standing in a circle, the women grasped hands. In unison with her sister and grandmother, Ivy whispered the chant, which she already knew by heart.

Kevin stared, his eyes wide, while the sheriff's narrowed eyes darted around the area as if he were looking for results. A delicate, warm breath of air stirred the forest floor. It wound through the trees around the gathered group and was gone, leaving a heavy feeling of anticipation in its wake. As the women continued to chant, a soft glow lit the base of the tree where Audrey had planted the coins.

Kevin tapped the sheriff's shoulder and pointed into the woods just to his right. A few feet away, a rock shimmered brilliantly, breaking the shroud of darkness. An incandescent mark shaped like a handprint adorned a tree just beyond that. Other lights emerged slowly from the darkness in the distance.

"Thank you," Audrey said from behind them.

Kevin turned to her, an astonished smile on his face. "That's where he went."

"Yes," Audrey confirmed.

"Amazing," Sheriff Owens whispered to himself. "Let's go," he said, snapping back to reality and his bold demeanor.

They followed the glowing objects through the woods. The link seemed tenuous, and it continued to fade as they moved farther away from the large maple tree. The group followed as quickly as possible under the tenebrous sky lit only by the stars. As the trees thinned, a small house appeared. Its shabby white paint reflected what little starlight it could gather through overgrown shrubbery and grass. A rusty windmill heavy with honeysuckle vines squeaked in the light breeze that wasn't strong enough to make the blades turn.

"What is this place?" Kevin asked no one in particular.

"It's the old Edgar farm. Jack's great-uncle lived here," Audrey said. "I don't know for sure who owns it now. We don't."

The sheriff turned and whispered to the women to stay back. He and Kevin started to approach the house, their firearms drawn.

"Wait," Ivy said.

They stopped abruptly and turned to her. She pointed to an open space beyond the house, where a large, crumbling barn stood partially hidden among the trees. "He'll be in the barn," she said, feeling certain. "If this is about me and he's recreating what Charlie couldn't finish, he'll be in that barn."

As if in response to Ivy's assertion, a light—visible through the cracks between the warped boards—flickered on inside the barn.

"Let's go," Audrey said.

"What makes you think that he won't tear you apart?" the sheriff asked.

In response, Audrey and Violet each pulled a small stone hung from a cord around her neck from under her shirt. Ivy thrust out her wrist, displaying a similar talisman on a corded bracelet. Hers was newer—Audrey had replaced it just the day before.

"We have protection," Audrey said. "And he hasn't gotten us so far. Ivy wasn't wearing it when he took her."

"That's why he didn't completely rip me apart when we found Ivy in that house," Violet said. "And Kevin…"

Sheriff Owens looked to Kevin for an explanation. Kevin held out his wrist, still wearing the bracelet Violet had given him.

"Okay, fine," Sheriff Owens said, exasperated. He threw up his hands and let them drop, clearly fed up with trying to protect people who were dead set against it. "Let's all go."

They crept toward the barn, though Ivy suspected Charlie already knew they were there. Yards from the crumbling structure, she felt the pressure of magic wrapping it.

When she realized the others were no longer at her side, she turned to find them still near the edge of the trees. They all stared at her. Violet's face was contorted in anger, and Audrey looked simply sad. Kevin shouted something that she could not hear, while the sheriff strained forward as if throwing his shoulder against a glass door. She turned back to the barn. Its door had opened. Dreadful comprehension pinched her heart. He'd set his trap—and she had walked into it.

She looked back at her grandmother and sister once more. Violet was shouting and beating her fists against the same invisible force that had stopped Sheriff Owens. Frowning, her eyes tearful, Audrey simply nodded as if telling Ivy to go and do what needed to be done.

Ivy faced the barn and went inside. A few naked bulbs in rusty sockets hung from the beams above, and bales of hay were stacked along the walls. Across from her, Charlie Logan waited, his red eyes staring her down. The hanging lights revealed what the darkness outside had hidden. His body was smooth and covered in burns that looked as though they had healed over more quickly than normal. Next to him stood Gillian Fuller, dwarfed by his massive presence. She seemed to have succumbed to the same spell he'd used to get Ivy to Libby Walsh's house. The door banged shut, and Ivy whirled to see a board drop into place, barring the door. *Oh, hell!*

"Oh, Ivy…" he said in the unearthly, sepulcher voice that floated in the air around him, drawing her attention back to him. His guttural tone disgusted her. As he admired his prize, he reached out slowly to touch the little girl's coppery hair. He goaded Ivy to come toward the girl, toward him. "She's so much more beautiful than you were."

Ivy shuddered inside but forced her muscles to be still.

His head snapped to the side so that he was looking straight at her. Despite a wince, Ivy stood her ground. His twisted facial features leered at her. His eyes shone. When Ivy gave no reaction, he turned back to the girl. He hunkered down in front of her and stroked her hair as he gathered a fistful of her cornflower-blue nightgown.

Ivy carefully reached behind herself and pulled the white-handled knife from the sheath at the small of her back. "You are so much uglier than Charlie was," Ivy said, still concealing the knife.

"You think so?" His mocking laughter reverberated against the walls of the barn as he threw back his head. He released the girl with such vehemence that she tottered backward over a hay bale and into the pile of loose hay behind it.

Ivy saw the perfect time to strike with the girl shielded at least a little behind the solid hay bale. As Charlie turned toward Ivy again, the smell of musty earth nearly overpowered her nostrils. Hypnotized by the hatred in his eyes, she hesitated for a heartbeat. Hate seemed to leach out of the sockets with black tendrils of smoke. Before she realized, he was far too close to her. He towered over her, but he was stooped as if preparing to envelop her into himself.

Startled, she jumped forward, propelled by anxiety, fear, and the desperate need to end him. He reacted too slowly. Before he could reach out to block her advance, Ivy plunged the blade of the knife into the side of his neck. He roared with pain as she pushed the knife across his neck, splitting a wide, glowing-red gash along his tight skin. His flailing arm smacked against Ivy's shoulder, pushing her down into the rotting hay and the powdery dirt that covered the floor of the barn. The knife still in Ivy's hand, she and Charlie fell together, and his weight pinned her beneath him. He grasped her neck as if to choke her. Then his talon-like fingernails grated down her shoulder, dragging deep into her upper arm. His nails felt as if they scraped bone, and she stifled a scream, biting down on the pain.

He gripped her face in his hand, puncturing the skin underneath her chin with his thumbnail, and forced her to meet his gaze. As she came face to face with him, Ivy didn't dare breathe. No sound escaped his gaping mouth. Wretched black smoke poured from the wound in his neck. She drew in a half sob that she forced away before another could follow. Clenching the knife tightly behind his back, Ivy struggled to push its point into his flesh again, but she couldn't bend her wrist enough to penetrate any farther. She squeezed her eyes shut and twisted her body away from him, letting go of the knife. Blood—her blood—had already soaked into the dry hay next to her. Her left hand, groping blindly in loose hay, touched something metal. She grasped it and pulled it toward her as Charlie continued to squeeze her throat.

Yanking the metal loose from the debris, she recognized the tines of a pitchfork missing its wooden handle. As her vision started to fade, she clutched the fork and tucked it in close to her belly, the tines facing outward. With everything she had left, she shoved the fork into Charlie's stomach as he pressed down on her. His body sank onto the rusty metal points. Only the metal shaft held his slumped body away from her. The weight of his body forced the shaft a few centimeters into the loose dirt beside her torso. His grip on her throat loosened, and the fierce light in his eyes dimmed. Still, his fingers tangled in her hair, pulling her face closer to his. Their noses touched. She gasped, desperately drawing air into her lungs. She could no longer avoid inhaling his odor. He smelled of stale tobacco smoke and decomposing flesh. His mouth opened, and she thought for a second that he meant to devour her.

Gritting her teeth against the pain in her shoulder, she wrenched the blade from his back and stabbed it in deeper, twisting as far as her range of motion would allow. A low, deep hiss escaped his lips, and the light in his eyes went out completely. Ivy managed to shuffle out from beneath him after his body went limp. She scrambled up and pulled herself away from him. Dark smoke leaked out from around the hilt of the knife, dissipating into the shadowy barn.

She forced herself to breathe slowly. A soft whimpering came from the corner near the door, and she suddenly remembered that she was not alone with that monster in the barn. Afraid to take her eyes off the now-motionless shape in front of her, she backed toward the sound. She knew that the girl must have been shaken from her trance.

When she was closer, Ivy felt the little girl grab her shirt. "Is he dead?" Gillian whispered with a squeak.

Ivy pulled Gillian to her and hugged her tightly. Pieces of hay clinging to the girl's hair scratched at Ivy's neck as she lifted the girl. Ivy's arms were tired, but she squeezed the little girl to her even more tightly.

"I think so." Ivy's eyes still didn't leave the motionless figure on the ground.

An electrical hiss sizzled through the space between them, and the little girl tensed, burrowing her face into Ivy's shirt. The hiss was followed by smoke. Then a small spark spread into a growing fire. Sparks popped all around them, and the body went up in flames, licking at the dry hay.

"Oh, we have to go now." Searching for an exit, she settled on a barred door. She put the girl down so that she could open the door. "Stay right here."

Ivy hefted the rotted board out of its hook and let it fall to the ground with a hollow clatter. She jerked hard on the rusted handle, but the door didn't budge. Pressing her ear against the wood, Ivy thought she could hear voices outside over the roar and crackle of the fire behind her.

"Help!" Gillian shrieked at the top of her lungs. Together, she and Ivy beat at the door, calling for help.

"It won't open," Ivy shouted.

A pounding from the outside answered. She glanced back at the fire, gagging on smoke. Charlie's body burned with an unearthly flame, her knife still lodged in his back. Urgency outweighed the temptation to go back for it.

Grimacing, she rubbed her dirty hand over her bleeding shoulder. With her own blood, she scrawled the symbol for freedom on the door. Laying her palm over it, she willed every shred of her desperation into the door. It sprang loose, and she pushed it the rest of the way. Gillian reached out to her, and Ivy hauled the little girl out of the barn. Right outside, Sheriff Owens caught Gillian up in his arms and carried her as they ran from the fire and toward the trees.

They stopped just within the tree line, and all of them stared at the barn. Smoke poured from the windows, blending into the dark sky but blotting out the stars. And flames licked through the windows, bathing the trees around them in an eerie red glow. Gillian slipped her small, clammy hand into Ivy's, and Ivy pulled her closer. She glanced down at the girl, whose eyes were wide pools reflecting the flames. Ivy turned back to fire. The burning barn filled her with surprising satisfaction, so much so that she regretted not having burnt her grandmother's barn ages ago.

Suddenly, a boom rocked the earth. A roar of wind hit Ivy's back, shoving her forward. She dropped to the ground, covering Gillian. Overhead, the wind seemed to howl with mournful moans. Ivy made out the outline of a face, its eyes wide in panic, in the silvery shapes streaking toward the fire. The shapes coursed through the darkness from every direction. The barn seemed to swallow them as soon as they converged upon the structure.

Gillian raised her head, but Ivy covered it with her arms. "No. Don't look," she said into the girl's ear.

Next to her, Kevin was clutching Violet, his eyes squeezed shut. Violet looked over at Ivy with wide eyes. Then it was over. The roar of the burning barn seemed like silence compared to the howling wind.

"What the hell? Did anybody else see that?" Sheriff Owens shouted, jumping to his feet. "Holy hell!"

Ivy got to her feet then helped Gillian stand. Everyone seemed to be ignoring the sheriff's question. He stood looking around, a dumbfounded expression on his face, his arms spread out to the side as if he might catch an answer if it fell from the sky.

Ivy turned find her grandmother staring into the trees. "Gran?"

Shaking her head, Audrey met Ivy's gaze. "I don't know. Something must have opened up—or closed. That was big."

"So you saw?" Sheriff Owens said. "Jesus, I thought I was losing my mind. This case… I just don't *know* anymore."

When Gillian squeezed her hand, Ivy knelt to look the girl in the eye. Soot and dirt streaked the girl's face and hung in her hair. She was still barefoot, standing in the underbrush of the woods.

Ivy smiled weakly.

"Can I see my mom?" Gillian asked. Tears welled up in her eyes, but she swallowed hard and put on a brave face.

"Of course," Ivy answered, hugging her again. The sheriff was still staring dumbly at the barn, so she looked to Kevin, who nodded even as he was pulling out his cell phone.

"Sheriff, I'm gonna call this in, okay?" Kevin said extra loudly to get the sheriff's attention. "Call the fire department, too?"

"Yeah. Yeah!" He threw his hands in the air. "Yeah, we gotta get this girl home." The sheriff patted Gillian's hand. "Sorry, sweetie."

Kevin paced, holding his phone to his ear with one hand, gesturing with his other while talking. He looked up at Ivy and nodded. "Yeah, definitely an ambulance, too. I've got two injured. And the suspect is inside the burning structure."

Ivy remembered her shoulder and realized one of the injured people was her. *How could I have forgotten that?* Suddenly more exhausted than she remembered ever being in her life, Ivy ached to her very bones. After a second of consideration, she forced herself to look down at her arm. Her tattered, bloody shirtsleeve was matted over the wound, making it difficult to discern any actual gore, especially in the dark. Just the thought of peeling away the cloth and dried blood made her wince. *At least it isn't still bleeding.*

Then, as if from nowhere, Violet appeared and wrapped her arms around both Ivy and Gillian. "It's okay, Ivy," she whispered, putting her hand gently over her sister's shredded sleeve.

Overwhelmed by the sudden urge to sit, Ivy let Violet lower her to the ground. Gillian, who seemed unwilling to part with Ivy, sat next to her, curled under her good arm.

"He's gone, though, right?" Ivy asked, looking up at Violet.

Violet nodded. "Yeah."

Ivy intended to close her eyes for just a second, to block out the stinging smoke, but she succumbed to her weariness before she realized it had swallowed her.

Epilogue

I VY WOKE TO THE UNFAMILIAR creaking of the tenant house. She wasn't used to its feel yet. Beverly and the girls had done a house swap after Beverly decided that she could do with a little more company than the empty house offered her. Ivy had agreed that having more space to herself suited her better than sharing the farmhouse with her grandmother. Still, she sometimes missed the feel of her grandmother nearby, though she could see the farmhouse just through her bedroom window. Ivy suspected Bev had wanted to be away from the place that held so many memories but no longer held the man she'd made the memories with.

For a moment, still bleary, she stared at the dark silhouette on her nightstand. As the outline resolved into the bouquet of flowers that Mark Morrison had sent her, Ivy smiled. She was looking forward to officially starting her new job on Monday.

The get-well card and flowers might have been standard business for Mark, but no one had ever done that for Ivy before. If he'd known where to send the flowers, he must have realized who she was. Ivy decided she didn't care, though. He and Karen had been nothing but nice to her, just like the other people in town. Hanna Gordon had come to visit, and Mrs. Fuller had brought Gillian to the farm. Maybe these people, not Rachel Grant, were the ones who made her magic.

The smell of coffee floated up the stairs to where Ivy lay in bed. She rolled over to face the window, expecting to see the early-morning sun peeking around the edges of the curtains. Instead, the sky was still dark beyond her window. She bolted upright as her skin tingled with the feeling that an unexpected presence was in the house. The visitor wasn't menacing or sinister, only unexpected.

Violet appeared in the open doorway, wrapped in a short blue robe with fuzzy flowers. "Come here," she whispered, beckoning her with a twitch of her fingers.

"What?" Ivy threw back the covers and got out of bed. She winced at the pain lingering in her shoulder. The doctor had promised the physical therapy would help heal the damaged tendons, but the nasty scar that was forming there would remind her of Charlie Logan long after the pain was gone. "Are you making coffee? It smells like coffee." She glanced at the blue glow of the alarm clock on her nightstand. It was barely four o'clock in the morning. Still, she quietly followed her sister into the hall.

"No, it's not me," Violet said as she led the way downstairs. "I don't know, but we might have a problem."

A wave of concern washed over her, but a familiar sound damped it—a spoon clinking against a coffee cup. A man's voice hummed quietly in the kitchen at the bottom of the stairs. Ivy recognized the melody of "Wildwood Rose" immediately.

Ivy and Violet stopped at the base of the stairs. Perplexed, Ivy looked at her sister.

Violet shrugged and shook her head. "Gran said Charlie opened something between worlds. Must've happened then."

A pale blue but practically solid specter roamed the kitchen, opening cabinets as if searching for something, while he hummed idly to himself. A cup of steaming coffee sat next to the sugar bowl on the table. "Nothing's where it's supposed to be. Where's she put the damn creamer now?" the apparition whispered to himself with a trace of exasperation.

Should have known Sam was too protective of Bev to ever leave her, even in death.

"Bev!" he called out, apparently unconcerned that it was four in the morning.

"We keep the creamer in the fridge," Violet said with a slight smile. The sisters had rearranged things when they moved in. Beverly and Sam had used the powdered creamer, but Ivy liked the liquid that belonged in the refrigerator.

The figure started and turned, flashing her a charming smile. He was the younger, fit Sam she remembered from years ago, not the Sam who'd been torn apart and left to die in the yard. "Hello, ladies," Sam said cheerfully.

"Would you care to join me for some morning coffee?" His eyes searched behind them expectantly. "Where's Bev?" *Oh, no. He doesn't know.*

Ivy looked to Violet, who simply raised her eyebrows and shrugged again.

"Oh, Sam," Ivy said quietly, sitting at the table, "We've got a lot to tell you."

Acknowledgments

I owe a great big thank-you to Jessica, Sarah, and the proofreading team at Red Adept Publishing.

Thank you to Drew, Kelsi, and Greg, who suffered through the roughest draft, and to Phillip, who suffered through every draft.

About the Author

Stefanie Spangler has always loved books and reading, and one day, she decided to write a book of her own.

Stefanie lives in central Illinois with her husband and daughters. When she's not reading or writing, she's usually editing someone else's book. But she also enjoys gardening, knitting, and forcing others to read her favorite books.